Alex leaned forward. "I think she's waiting for me to kiss you."

Tara's mouth went dry. "What?"

"You've heard of a kiss, haven't you, Mackey? It's when—"

"I know what a kiss is, Kirkland. And don't worry about it. You've gone above and beyond the call of duty today."

He slid his hand around the back of her neck. "I'd hate to disappoint Roxie. And if we're pretending we're on a date, we might as well put on a good show."

Before she could protest, he leaned forward and pressed his lips to hers. The kiss was light, soft, but it stirred a heat inside of her she hadn't experienced in a very long time.

He pulled back a few inches, but he was still close enough so that his warm breath brushed her face. "You think that's enough to convince Roxie?"

Her heart hammered against her ribs. It wasn't enough for her. "Yes."

A slight smile tipped the edge of his mouth. "Maybe one more, just for good measure."

Dear Reader,

I've always been humbled and intrigued by those dedicated individuals who reopen cold cases. Often they are the most skilled in their fields and are driven by a sense of obligation to the forgotten victims and their families who've been denied closure and justice. Forensic technology, the passage of time or a lucky break are often just the right sparks they use to heat up a cold case.

Tara and Alex—the reporter and the cop—are two such people. Though they often find themselves at cross-purposes in their daily professional lives, both are driven by a strong sense of justice and are willing to put everything on the line to solve a case.

As you snuggle up on a cold winter night, I hope you enjoy Tara and Alex's journey through the streets of Boston and up the coast of Maine as they dig into the unsolved mystery of a missing heiress.

Have a very happy New Year!

Mary Burton

COLD CASE COP

Mary Burton

ISBN-13: 978-0-373-27568-7
ISBN-10: 0-373-27568-4

COLD CASE COP

This edition published by arrangement with Harlequin Books S.A.

Visit Silhouette Books at www.eHarlequin.com

Printed in U.S.A.

Books by Mary Burton

Silhouette Romantic Suspense

In Dark Waters #1378
The Arsonist #1410
Wise Moves #1426
Cold Case Cop #1498

Harlequin Historical

A Bride for McCain #502
The Colorado Bride #570
The Perfect Wife #614
Christmas Gold #627
"Until Christmas"
Rafferty's Bride #632
The Lightkeeper's Woman #693
The Unexpected Wife #708
Heart of the Storm #757

MARY BURTON

published her first book, a historical western romance in 1999 and in 2005 was a Romance Writers of America RITA® Award finalist for *The Unexpected Wife*. *Cold Case Cop* is her sixteenth book.

Burton is a graduate of Hollins University and currently lives in Virginia. Hobbies include yoga, the occasional triathlon, and she volunteers as a kitchen assistant in a culinary school. She is working on her eighteenth novel.

For the Virginia Romance Writers

Chapter 1

Monday, July 14, 9:00 a.m.

Catcalls from the homicide squad room had Sergeant Alex Kirkland looking up through the glass walls of his office. His gaze skimmed past the six grinning detectives and settled on a tall, leggy redhead who stopped to greet each person in the room.

Tara Mackey.

A visit from the *Boston Globe*'s crime beat reporter meant his first day back on the job wouldn't be as quiet as he'd hoped. But it would be interesting.

Grinning, Mackey wore her trademark getup—

dark dress pants, a snugly fitting crisp white shirt and a severe ponytail tied at the base of her skull that accentuated high cheekbones. Some of the detectives called her The Librarian. But Mackey was anything but dowdy or ordinary. She had a killer figure, full lips and a spark in her green eyes that always had Kirkland's body tensing.

Mackey was a Bostonian by birth but had gotten her start in journalism in Washington, D.C. She'd worked for the *Post* for eight years. She had returned to Boston to work the crime beat less than a year ago. She covered every homicide, regardless of the time of day or social status of the victim, and she had gotten to know all the names of the division detectives on both the day and night shifts. The cops didn't always like her hard-hitting questions, but they liked her. Intelligent articles combined with overly sensational headlines had earned her a following in the city.

Closing the file on last night's homicide report, Alex rose and allowed a second sweep of his gaze over her body. Too bad he didn't date reporters.

Mackey broke away from the detectives and came into his office. She moved well. "Welcome back."

Alex shoved his hands in his pockets and rattled the loose change in his left pocket. "What do you want, Mackey?"

Tara's grin reached her eyes. She was clearly unaffected by his gruffness. In fact, she seemed to get a kick out of irritating him. "I see your near-death experience hasn't improved your social graces, Kirkland."

Her direct reference to his near-fatal shooting caught him off guard. No one except the department's shrink had directly discussed the ambush with him. His injuries reminded family, friends and especially other cops that a policeman's job was very dangerous. Very aware of this, he had, in the days leading up to his return to work, spent extra time sailing his boat on the bay so that the sun tanned his skin until it had regained its healthy glow. He'd lifted weights at the gym to build up his muscles. And this morning he'd taken additional time dressing.

Alex was aware that the cops in the squad room were listening, even if their gazes were averted. He moved to his office door and closed it. "Did you come to talk to me about manners?"

She laughed. "No. May I sit?"

It was a great laugh. "Sure."

Mackey made herself comfortable in the chair that was positioned in front of his desk. She crossed those long legs as he moved behind her and around to his chair. He realized she'd changed her perfume. No longer spicy, this scent was soft and feminine. He liked it. A lot.

He sat behind his desk. "So you came all this way to welcome me back to work? I'm touched, Mackey."

"Park your ego, sport. I'm here about an article."

"Really? And here I thought your visit was all about me."

"Not exactly."

"I didn't think so." His swivel chair squeaked as he leaned back.

She dug a file out of her slim briefcase. "I'm embarking on a new project."

"And I should care why?"

"It directly affects one of your old cases."

"An old case? I'm up to my ass in alligators, including three new homicides last night alone. Today is not a good day to discuss new projects or old cases."

A few of his men gawked at Mackey through his office's glass walls. Irritated, he glared at them. They all had the sense to get back to work.

"I won't take too much of your time, Kirkland. Besides, you owe me."

Alex folded his arms over his chest. "Is that a fact?"

She cocked her head. "When you asked the media to write a series of articles on those vagrant murders three months ago, everyone turned you down but me. And as I remember, you got an arrest because of the tips *my* article generated."

Kirkland had broken the case because of her help. "The fact that you stepped up to the plate then is the reason I haven't thrown you out yet. But my patience is wearing thin."

Mackey laid an inch-thick file of news clips in the

center of his desk. "I've decided to do a little digging into one of your department's cold cases."

The muscles in his back tightened as they always did when trouble lurked too close. "Which case?"

She smiled and paused for dramatic effect. "Kit Westgate Landover. Remember her?"

"How could I forget? You couldn't have picked a more volatile case."

"I know."

Kit had been a West-Coast socialite who'd taken Boston society by storm two years ago. After landing the city's most eligible, albeit much older, bachelor, she'd vanished during her wedding reception a year ago. The huge affair had been held at the Landover estate and had been the social event of the season. Over five pints of Kit's blood, enough to kill anyone, had been found splattered all over the estate's greenhouse. However, no body had been found. "Why are you digging into this case, Mackey?"

Her eyes brightened with excitement. "Why wouldn't I? When a rich, beautiful woman vanishes, it's big news. This story ate up headlines for months."

Because of the endless news stories, the brass and Kit's new husband, Pierce Landover, had screamed for the cops to find Kit and to make an arrest. Kirkland and a half-dozen other cops had worked nonstop for months. But there'd been no sign of Kit or her killer. "Pierce Landover won't appreciate this."

If she were concerned, she didn't show it. "I can handle him."

Kirkland shook his head. "Landover went to the mayor and then to the governor to have me fired when I couldn't crack the case. My arrest record and a few connections of my own barely saved my ass."

Her eyes narrowed a fraction. "Can you confirm that you think that Kit's dead?"

He drummed his fingers on his desk. "I didn't say that. We never did determine what happened to Mrs. Landover." And that fact still bothered him. He hated unsolved cases. "Look, Mackey, the Boston Police Department has a dozen homicides pending right now—cases *with bodies*. If you want to play Nancy Drew cover one of them."

She ignored him. "Care to have a peek at a mock-up of next week's Metro section?"

Alex watched as she dipped long fingers into her briefcase. "Why do I have the feeling I won't like this?"

"You may really love it." Her voice had a throaty quality that had him wondering what else she might love. "My articles have helped you solve cases before."

"Let's have it."

She laid the Metro section in front of him. "This is how I envision the story laying out. A friend of mine in production did it for me."

Above the fold was a full-color picture of Kit Landover. The woman was stunning. In her late twenties, she had that magical combination of womanly confidence and flawless looks. Her hypnotic gaze stared at the camera lens as if she knew a secret that everyone else wanted to know.

It had been two years since he'd seen Kit in the flesh. She'd arrived at a gallery opening on Pierce Landover's arm, and had immediately stopped conversation. An indigo silk halter dress had clung to her high, full breasts, small waist and sizzling, tight body. Rich blond curls, parted on the side, had accentuated seductively high cheekbones and enhanced violet eyes.

Every man in the room had entertained erotic fantasies. Every woman in the room had oozed resentment.

Alex flipped the paper over and read the bold headline just below the fold. It read Socialite's Disappearance Still Unsolved After One Year—Paper Seeking Tips. He shoved out a breath. "You're opening a hornets' nest, Mackey."

Two slim gold bracelets jangled on her wrist as she ran a hand over her ponytail. "That was the idea. Anniversaries have a way of stirring things up, and I'm hoping this mock-up shakes people up and gets them talking to me. After a year, I'm banking on the fact that someone will remember something about Kit they hadn't shared a year ago."

He laid the paper down. "Do yourself a favor and drop this case."

The glint in Mackey's eyes told him his warning

had fallen on deaf ears. "Do you have any theories on what happened to Kit?"

Tension rippled through his muscles. "I don't comment on open cases."

"Murder. Killing. Open. It's not like you to be so unguarded, Kirkland. You must have a theory on this case."

He didn't usually make rookie mistakes around reporters. He stiffened and frowned. "Don't use my words against me."

She leaned forward, matching his glare. "There is more to this story, Kirkland. I can feel it."

If he dropped his gaze a fraction he'd have a clear view of her cleavage. "What made you choose this story?"

She shrugged and glanced at her mock-up. "I've had the idea to do a cold-case article for a while. And the Kit Westgate case seemed the perfect choice."

His gaze dropped to her breasts. Nice. He moved his gaze to her pale face and the faint sprinkle of freckles on her nose. "Find another case."

She straightened. "No can do, Sergeant."

"I've given you a friendly warning. Stay out of this." But she was right. There was more to Kit's disappearance, only he hadn't been able to figure out what *it* had been.

She grinned. "Kirkland, please. Since when have I ever listened to your warnings?"

He almost laughed at that one. "Never."

"Exactly."

Mackey possessed a spark—a vitality—that made other women uninteresting. "Whoever was involved in Kit's murder or disappearance covered their tracks carefully. You're not going to shake anyone up with a mock-up."

She rose as if sensing she'd get nothing more out of him. She picked up her briefcase. Her fingers were long, but her nails were neatly trimmed, unpolished and not fussy. "We'll see. I'm betting something does happen."

Rising, Alex ran his hand down his tie. "You're a good, solid reporter, Mackey. Why stoop to a sensational case like this one?"

She frowned. "Regardless of her social standing, something bad happened to Kit Westgate Landover. And she deserves justice."

He rubbed the back of his neck. "Come on, this isn't really about *justice*. This is about headlines and advancing your career."

She leaned forward, giving him a better view of her breasts. "Sure. I won't lie. The headlines are a definite advantage. But I also want to know what happened to Kit."

"This is still an open investigation. If you find something, bring it to me. And if I find out you're holding back information, there's going to be trouble."

She smiled, moved toward his office door and rested her hand on the doorknob. "I would never hold back on you, Kirkland."

"That's a load of bull, and we both know it."

She laughed and opened the door.

He watched her walk toward the elevator and muttered an oath. Damn, but he did admire the way her hips swayed.

Alex had the feeling that all hell was about to break loose.

Chapter 2

Monday, July 14, 10:05 a.m.

Tara hadn't figured that Alex Kirkland would give a quote on this case. He was too good a cop to let his cards show. But she had got a sense of his frustration. It did bother him that Kit's case had never been solved.

And she couldn't resist seeing for herself that he was truly on the mend. She'd kept tabs on him while he was in the hospital recovering from the shooting that had shocked everyone.

Kirkland had been shot during a routine investigation. He and Detective Matthew Brady had gone to the home of a wealthy doctor to ask him questions about his wife's suspicious death. The doctor had answered the front door armed with a loaded shotgun. According to Brady, Kirkland had reacted instantly. He'd pushed Brady out of harm's way as he'd drawn his own gun. The doctor had fired, hitting Kirkland in the chest and thigh. The buckshot had nicked the femoral artery in his leg and punctured his lung. Kirkland had fallen to the ground but had fired his own weapon. The single shot had killed the doctor.

The entire exchange had happened in a split second, but Brady recognized that Kirkland was in bad shape. He was still conscious but in terrible pain and bleeding badly. Kirkland had nearly bled out before the paramedics got him to the hospital.

Three days after Kirkland's shooting, Tara had snuck onto the ICU floor at Boston General. She'd told the doctors she'd been checking on Kirkland's progress for a follow-up article on the shooting. They'd allowed her to peer through the glass walls of his room.

What she saw nearly took her breath away. He'd been lying in the hospital bed, as pale as his sheets and barely conscious. There'd been so many wires hooked up to him. The sight had shocked her. She'd not had the nerve to go into his room, but had lingered several feet back. The doctor had said that the injury would have killed most.

Now, despite the July heat, the memory still had the power to send chills down Tara's spine.

With an effort, she tried to focus on the fact that he looked good now. His tall, lean frame remained taught and muscular. Time in the sun had left his skin tanned and his newly cut brown hair a shade lighter. He looked good. Real good.

She parallel-parked her beat-up white Toyota on the exclusive, tree-lined Beacon Hill side street. This exclusive area of Boston screamed old money and privilege. And it set her nerves on edge.

She shut off the car engine. She didn't do well with snobby, rich people. They made her feel awkward and somehow *less* because she didn't have blue blood in her veins. Intellectually, she understood this was stupid, a reaction to a sad episode in her past, but no amount of inner pep talks quite erased her feeling of inferiority.

Skimming fingers over her ponytail, she reminded herself that she'd been a reporter for nine years and had interviewed some of the most powerful and dangerous people in Washington, D.C. and Boston. She'd written about politicians, murderers, arsonists and sophisticated white-collar crooks. An old rich guy living on Beacon Hill wasn't going to throw her off her game.

Tara pocketed her keys and grabbed her briefcase, slid out of the car and closed the door. Halfway down the block her cell phone rang. She dug the phone out of her purse. Caller ID confirmed it was her editor, Miriam Spangler.

Tara flipped the phone open. "I am on my way to Landover's as we speak, Miriam."

"Remember, don't piss him off." Miriam's voice was gruff, a product of thirty years of chain smoking. "His family is as powerful as the Kennedy clan. Rile him up and there could be hell to pay."

That comment irritated Tara. "I can handle myself, Miriam."

"You do have a temper, sweetie. It's why you left D.C."

"It's one of the reasons I left D.C. And I've learned my lesson."

As if she hadn't spoken, Miriam said, "Don't push this too hard. If Landover says to drop it, drop it."

Tara's blood shot past the boiling point in a second. "Yesterday you were salivating when I showed you the mock-up of the article and pitched the idea."

Miriam blew smoke into the receiver. "I had all night and most of this morning to conjure a thousand devastating scenarios in my head. Most of them included me without a job or a pension. If and when this article runs, it's going to be dicey."

Tara muttered a few choice words. "When did you get to be so timid?"

"Since I realized I'm two years away from collecting a full pension."

Frustration fueled Tara's anger. "My readership has been growing steadily, and this is the kind of story that will hit home with them. Remember, you gave me the go-ahead to look into Kit Westgate Landover's case."

"I know. I know."

"Think about it, Miriam. This is the stuff of Pulitzers. Network news coverage. Book deals. When I go to the top I'll be telling everyone you were the star editor behind me. I will make you famous and position you for your own book deal."

Miriam sighed. "We both know I didn't want to fade quietly into retirement."

She smiled, knowing she'd hit all Miriam's hot buttons. "Exactly."

"All right. Go for it. But please just be careful, Tara."

"I will be fine." Tara closed her cell and shoved it in her briefcase as she reached Landover's house. Standing on the sidewalk, she stared up at the corner-lot mansion. The home had been built in the seventeen hundreds and was steeped in history. This had always been an exclusive pricey area of Boston, but in today's market this place was worth a king's ransom.

She climbed the stone steps to the black, lacquered front door. A pineapple brass door knocker hung in the door's center.

Tara rapped the knocker twice against the massive

door. The sound echoed inside the house. She moistened her lips and stood a little straighter.

Miriam's and Kirkland's words nagged her as she tried not to fidget. They were right. She had a hot head. Back in D.C., she probably shouldn't have called that senator an idiot. But she was smart enough to learn from her mistakes. She could handle Pierce Landover if she could get in to see him.

Footsteps echoed in the hallway inside. If her luck held, she'd get Landover's maid, or someone else who didn't know her. She then might be able to get into the house and maybe see Landover. There'd been times in the past when she'd talked her way into situations and gotten great quotes.

But there'd also been times when she'd been tossed out and threatened with legal action.

That could be today's scenario if Cecilia Reston, Landover's personal assistant for the last twenty-five years, answered the door. Reston protected her employer with the ferocity of a bulldog. And she'd have no trouble reporting Tara to the cops.

Tara glanced at her black flats and, seeing dust on them, quickly rubbed them against the panty hose under her pant leg.

The door opened to a very young woman dressed in a maid's outfit. She had dark, straight hair pulled back with a rubber band and big brown eyes that telegraphed naïveté. "Yes?"

Tara smiled brightly. "I'm Tara Mackey. I have an appointment with Mr. Landover."

The young maid frowned as if confused. "I didn't realize he was seeing people today. Are you here about the clothes he's giving away?"

Tara wasn't sure what she was talking about. "Clothes?"

"His wife's clothes. He's giving all her gowns away to charity."

"Ah, yes. She had such stunning gowns. We have a ten-thirty appointment to discuss the gowns," she said without blinking.

The maid nodded and stepped aside. "If you'll wait here."

Tara's heart jumped, but she kept her cool as she stepped inside. "Thank you."

So Landover was giving away Kit's dresses. Was it a sign that the old man was moving on with his life?

The maid hurried up the carpeted spiral staircase and down the upstairs hallway. Her footsteps faded away. Tara was left alone in the foyer.

She studied the marbled foyer's black-and-white polished floor. A crystal chandelier hung from the ceiling and caught the morning sunlight, which streamed in through a transom above the door. Across from the door stood an antique Chippendale table pushed against the wall. On the table sat a Chinese vase filled with fragrant, freshly cut roses.

The understated decor was all very elegant and expensive and not to her taste at all. She liked simple and unpretentious pieces that were often used and had a quirky history.

To her left, a set of tall mahogany doors stood ajar, giving her a peek into the receiving parlor. Unable to resist, she moved to the open door and looked inside. Immediately her gaze was drawn to the huge painting of Kit that hung over the brick fireplace. In the portrait, Kit wore a soft pink strapless dress that cloaked her lithe body like a second skin. Her blond hair was swept up into a chignon, and a stunning diamond pendant necklace dipped into her full cleavage. Teardrop gems dangled from her ears, and a thick diamond bracelet circled her wrist. Tara recognized the gems in the portrait. They were the ones Kit had been wearing on her wedding day—the ones that had vanished with her and were reported to be worth fifteen million dollars.

Tara glanced up the staircase to see if anyone could see her. Satisfied that she was alone, she pulled out her cell phone, quickly snapped a picture.

The sound of footsteps on the landing had her stepping back into the foyer. She jammed her cell phone into her briefcase.

"May I help you?"

Tara turned to find a stern-looking woman descending the stairs. Dark brown hair was swept tightly back and accentuated sharp brown eyes. She wore a silk blouse, linen pants and high-heeled shoes.

"That's a stunning portrait of Mrs. Landover," Tara said. There was no sense hiding the fact that she'd been caught peeking.

The woman lifted a thin eyebrow as if she did not approve. "My name is Mrs. Reston. What can I do for you?"

Tara mentally regrouped. So much for getting in to see the old man today. "I'm Tara Mackey. I'm with the *Globe*. I spoke to you earlier about an appointment with Mr. Landover."

Mrs. Reston's lips flattened into a thin line. "I told you on the phone that Mr. Landover doesn't speak with reporters."

Tara smiled, trying not to look the least bit deterred. "I would only need about five or ten minutes of his time."

Mrs. Reston quickly slid a bony finger under her pearl necklace. "No."

"The one-year anniversary of his wife's disappearance is coming up next week." From her briefcase she pulled out the mock-up of her article. "The *Globe* is going to do a story about Kit Westgate. The hope is to spark the public's interest. Maybe someone will come forward with new information about what happened to Kit. Either way, we'd love Mr. Landover's comments for the piece."

Thin lips dipped into a frown as Reston stared at the glowing picture of Kit. Jealousy burned in her eyes. Reston had clearly hated Kit. "No reporter has cared a wit for Mr. Landover or all the good works he's done since Kit Westgate came into his life. Everyone just cared about her. Why can't your type leave him alone?"

The *your type* comment had Tara bristling, but she kept her cool. "I just want to ask him a couple of questions. I only need a few minutes of his time."

"I know Kit Westgate is just a story to you, but she devastated Mr. Landover's life. The woman was in league with the devil as far as I'm concerned. And frankly, I don't care if we ever find out what happened to her. Drop this story."

The show of emotion interested Tara. "You really hated her, didn't you?"

Mrs. Reston hesitated, realizing she'd let too much of her emotions show through her stoic Boston reserve. "Leave this house before I call the police and have you arrested for trespassing. And don't ever come back here or try to speak to Mr. Landover again."

Tara could just imagine Miriam's and Kirkland's expressions when word reached them that she'd been arrested for harassing Mrs. Reston. Kirkland's dark gaze was the hardest to banish.

Tara crossed the threshold to the front stoop. She turned. "Mrs. Reston, when was the last time you actually saw Kit?"

Mrs. Reston slammed the door in her face.

For a moment, Tara stood there, staring at the polished brass knocker just inches from her nose.

It wasn't even noon, and Kirkland, her editor and Landover's personal assistant had warned her off this story.

Why didn't they want the case reopened? Solving it would be a huge coup for the police and the paper. And it would bring resolution to Kit's family.

Tara shoved the newspaper into her briefcase and started toward her car. Her body tingled like it did when she felt as if she'd hit upon a great story.

She sensed that if she kept showing her mock-up around Boston she was going to coax a few hidden facts out of someone.

Smiling, Tara started to whistle as she slid behind the wheel and fired up the engine. She turned on the radio and cranked it loud. "There's no doubt about it. I'm on the right track."

Chapter 3

Monday, July 14, 10:45 a.m.

Tara was glad to leave the Beacon Hill district. She cut through side streets, winding her way north for several miles until she reached the north end.

This part of town always brought her blood pressure down. She loved the narrow, winding streets and the four-story brick apartment houses. No one here had a yard, and during summer evenings neighbors often set up chairs on the sidewalk to chat. The taverns had a homey feel to them. The shops were practical, not pretentious. The food was hearty and not gourmet. This was where the working class people lived.

She checked her notes to confirm Marco Borelli's address. Marco had been Kit's chauffeur—the one man besides her husband who'd spent the most time with her. There'd been reports that the two had often talked quietly to each other, and some rumors suggested they had been having an affair. However, nothing was ever proven.

Tara wove down a collection of side streets into a poorer section of town. She parked in front of an apartment house that looked in need of renovation.

She got out of the car and climbed the stairs to the front door. Close up, she could see that the black paint was peeling and the threshold was rotting. Mortar between the bricks was chipped, and there was a strong smell of garbage. She tried the front door and discovered it was locked.

Frustrated, she glanced to the call buttons on the left side of the door. It was doubtful Borelli would let her in, so she pushed several at once, hoping one of the residents upstairs would buzz her in. In a clear voice, she said into the intercom, "Pizza."

To her relief, the lock clicked open and she quickly entered the building.

Tara climbed the steps to the third floor. Her nose wrinkled at the blending smells of cabbage and trash. The hardwood floors on the steps were scarred and the banister was shaky enough to give way with the slightest amount of pressure. When she reached the third floor, she found apartment three-A and knocked.

No answer. She knocked again. "Mr. Borelli, are you home?"

Tara pressed her ear to the door and heard the faint sound of a TV game show. Someone was in there. She knocked again. "Mr. Borelli?"

Frustrated, she pulled a business card from her purse and wrote a quick note for him to call her. She tucked it in his doorjamb.

Tara was about to leave when Borelli's door snapped open. Her card fluttered to the floor.

A man stood in the doorway, his wide, muscled shoulders filling the door. He had coal-black hair slicked back off his face, a wide jaw and a muscular build accentuated by a tight black T-shirt. Diamond studs adorned each earlobe and a gold chain hung around his neck.

In the pictures she had of Borelli, he was always in the background behind Kit, and was always conservatively dressed in a dark suit. He was part chauffeur and part bodyguard. "Mr. Borelli?" Tara asked.

He frowned. "Maybe. Who wants to know?"

"I'm Tara Mackey. I have a few questions for you about Kit Westgate."

His scowl made his thick brow look heavier. "I don't talk to cops."

"I'm not a cop. I work for the *Boston Globe*. I'm a reporter."

His expression darkened, and she suspected he liked cops better than reporters. "I'm done talking with reporters, too. You all are a bunch of bloodsuckers, if you ask me. You vultures just about hounded me to death a year ago." He reached inside his apartment, grabbed a bag of garbage and then shouldered past her to the waste chute. His thick aftershave trailed after him.

"I am a fair reporter."

He snorted. "Right. Between the cops and the reporters, my life was hell. I ain't going back to that."

She peered into his apartment. The small room was furnished with a sofa and a TV. Her gaze skimmed past a half-eaten pizza on the lone coffee table, and over the floor littered with empty beer cans.

Her nose wrinkled. "Did you have a party?"

Borelli muttered an oath. "None of your business."

"Hey, I'm not here to cause you trouble. You were cleared by the cops of any wrongdoing in Kit's disappearance. You were in New York the day the Landovers married and she vanished."

He yanked the chute open and dumped the trash down. He released the door, and it banged against the wall. "That's right. I was hundreds of miles away."

"So it shouldn't be a big deal for you to answer a couple of questions. Five minutes of your time is all I ask."

He folded his arms over his chest. On his biceps there was a tattoo of a coiled snake holding a broken heart. "You're gonna twist my words like those other reporters did."

"I won't. I just want to hear your side of the story." And then, without waiting for a *no* answer, she said, "You used to live on the Landover estate, didn't you?"

He glanced at his buffed nails. "Yeah, I had a guest cottage near the garage."

"You must have had a sense of how Landover's relationship was going with Kit. Do you think he could have killed her?"

Borelli's face hardened. "Sure, he could have killed her. The guy had a temper, and I saw him slap Kit in the face once."

"You tell the cops?"

"I sure did." He leaned toward her, his tall frame towering over her. "Kit was afraid of Pierce. And I think she'd have backed out of the marriage if she could have. But she was afraid to."

"She told you she was afraid?"

"Yeah. A couple of times." He was a hard one to read.

"Why would Mr. Landover kill Kit on their wedding day? Especially with half the world watching."

Borelli shrugged. "Who the hell knows? Rich people are different than the rest of us. All I know is that they fought often those last few weeks. Even on their wedding day they got into it. You hear a lot when you're sitting in the front seat of a car."

"What did they fight about?"

"Anything and everything. Mostly, he just didn't like the way she flirted with other men. And she didn't like being told what to do."

This was a side of Kit she'd never heard about. "Did she flirt with anyone in particular?"

"Naw. She just liked men. And she really enjoyed wrapping them around her finger." He frowned as if a memory jabbed at him. Abruptly, he moved around her to the threshold of his apartment. "I've said what I'm going to say. You're making me miss *Wheel of Fortune*."

Tara thought about the pictures she'd collected of Kit during her research. A sharp intelligence burned behind her sapphire eyes. "What about the missing gems? She was wearing fifteen million in ice when she vanished. Any theories on that?"

"How would I know? I'm guessing that whoever killed her must have taken them." He leaned against the door frame, letting his gaze trail over her body. A smile played at the edge of his mouth.

When Kirkland's gaze had glided over her this morning, she'd felt a thrill of desire. This guy gave her the creeps. "She was from California?"

"Yeah. Northern California. Wine country."

"Did she ever keep up with anyone from her past?"

"Kit wasn't the type that looked back."

"If Pierce didn't kill her, any thoughts on who else might have murdered her?"

"If I knew, I'd have told the cops. But I still say that it was Landover." He flexed his biceps and the snake appeared to move. "So why you asking all these questions now? Kit's yesterday's news."

"She was a beautiful woman and she died young, like Marilyn Monroe or Anna Nicole Smith. People never get tired of hearing about those women. Even after years, their deaths are still shrouded in conspiracy theories."

"You're wrong. Kit's *old* news. Nobody cares about a spoiled, dead socialite."

She tried to keep her voice casual. "You said *dead socialite*. So you're sure she's dead."

He paused a beat to gather his thoughts. "She has to be dead. All that blood. No one could have survived."

"No body was found," she prompted.

Borelli grinned and, leaning forward, whispered, "Disposing of bodies is easy, lady. Just takes a few garbage bags and a saw."

A shudder ran through her body. She'd interviewed enough career criminals to recognize one. "You speaking from firsthand experience?"

He winked at her. "My advice to you is butt out. Or you might end up like Kit."

Her stomach knotted with tension, but she held her ground. "That a threat?"

Borelli smiled. A gold incisor glittered. "Friendly warning. Now go find yourself another story and stay out of my life." He retreated into the apartment, slamming the door behind him.

Tara stared at the closed door and dug her hand through her hair. "Not exactly a home run, but it's a start."

She checked her watch. She had time for one more interview before her shift at the bar where she worked nights. She had taken a sizable pay cut to move north. Reporting now barely kept a roof over her head, and she needed the second job to pay off the mountain of student loans from college.

Reston and Borelli had been difficult but she suspected her next interview was going to be worse. She had to find a way to get into the exclusive Founders' Yacht Club and speak to some of Kit's old friends.

She'd not been to the club in a long time, and didn't relish returning.

Alex spent the better part of the morning trying to forget Tara. But her visit had awakened so many unanswered questions that lingered from the Kit Westgate case.

He paced his office floor, ignoring the ache in his leg. Tara had said she was going to talk to Pierce. But he knew she would never get past Landover's assistant. Mrs. Reston had made hardened cops cringe. And if Tara thought she'd get quotes from any of the old man's friends, she was also mistaken. Boston society was an elite, closed group that didn't like airing dirty laundry.

But Alex could step into Landover's exclusive world. He'd been born into one of the wealthiest families in the state. He'd done his undergrad at Princeton and earned his law degree from Harvard. He'd been groomed to take over the Kirkland empire. And then his cousin had been slain by a mugger. The incident had rocked the family and changed the direction of his life. He'd quit the family business and joined the police force. The decision had cost him personally. His wife, Regina, hadn't understood the decision and had left him. His parents and brother were also furious with him. Even now his relationship with his family was strained.

But he'd never regretted his decision for a moment. He belonged in the police department.

Alex dialed Detective Brady's extension. Seconds later, the cop appeared at his door. "What do you need, Sergeant?"

Rising, Alex put the brunt of his weight on his good leg. "I'm going out for an hour or two. I want to follow up on a lead associated with the Kit Westgate case."

"You have a lead after a year?" Brady sounded surprised. "What is it?"

"Let me chase it down first. It most likely won't play out."

"No problem." Brady offered a crooked smile. "This got anything to do with Tara Mackey showing up here this morning?"

Alex wondered when he'd become so transparent. "Unfortunately, yes. She's going to do a piece on the anniversary of Kit's disappearance."

"Jeez. That's all we need."

"To her credit, she raised a few good questions."

Brady shook his head as if he were talking to one of his own five sons. "She's trouble."

Alex opened his desk drawer, pulled out his .38 and slid it into the gun holster on his belt. "Tell me what I don't know. But I've got to do a little nosing around just to settle my own doubts."

Brady's barrel chest filled with a deep breath. "You don't want me to ride along? I could drive."

The two men had only spoken about the shooting once. Brady had tried to show his gratitude over Kirkland saving him by way of an awkward thank-you. But Kirkland's own guilt over not being quicker on the draw had made it impossible for him to really discuss the incident. If he'd been a second slower, those five Brady boys wouldn't have a father. "Thanks. But I got it covered. I'll be back by lunch."

"Sure thing, boss."

It took Alex thirty minutes to cut through the city traffic and reach the exclusive Founders' Yacht Club located on Dorchester Bay. The club was one of the oldest in the state and had been a familiar spot for Kit and Pierce during their courtship.

Alex always felt as if he were stepping back in time when he drove through the club's brick-and-iron gates. Manicured lawns and discreet hedges lined the driveway that took him to the circle in front of the club's entrance. The two-story building was made of white marble and had large white columns. Large sections of the exterior were covered with neatly trimmed ivy.

A parking attendant glanced at Alex's police-issue Impala as if he weren't sure what to make of it or Alex. But then he got a look at Alex's face and relaxed. "Mr. Kirkland. Are you going sailing today?"

"No. This is a quick trip." Alex left the keys in the ignition and the engine running. "I'll be back in twenty minutes, so you might not want to park it in the annex lot."

"Right. Thanks."

Alex made his way up the stairs until he came face-to-face with a tall bear of a man. Dressed in a dark suit, white shirt and red tie, the man stood by the front door behind the reservation table, guarding the front gate of the club like a centurion.

"Danny," Alex said.

The man's stern face softened the instant his gaze met Alex's. "Mr. K. How are you doing?"

Alex liked Danny. "Good, Danny. How's that brother of yours?"

"Staying out of trouble," he said, lowering his voice. "Thanks for the talking-to you gave him. I can assure you that he won't be a problem again."

When Danny's brother Frankie had been arrested, the doorman had called Alex in a panic. Alex had pulled the kid out of holding and then taken him for a personal tour of the jail. By the time their visit had ended, the fourteen-year-old was pale, desperate to go home and vowing never to shoplift again.

Alex shoved his hand in his pocket. "I'm glad to hear that. Is my grandmother here?"

His grandmother, Gertrude Elizabeth Kirkland, and her four oldest friends met each Monday for a very serious game of gin rummy. The ladies could afford to bet big and they always did. But no matter who won or lost, the pot always went to St. Michael's Children's Charities.

Danny nodded. "She and the ladies are at their regular table."

"Thanks."

Danny glanced at Alex's open collar. "Excuse me, Mr. K., but you don't have a tie."

Alex reached for his collar. He'd taken his tie off

after Mackey had left because it had suddenly felt so confining. "I left it in my desk."

"You got to have a tie in the main room."

"I know." As a teenager, Alex had hated the club's mandatory tie rule. These days, remembering those petty rebellions made him smile. "Do you have an extra one that I could borrow?"

Danny smiled as he pulled a red tie out from under his desk and handed it to Alex. "How's that?"

"Perfect." Alex wrapped the tie around his neck and quickly wound it into a Windsor knot.

In the main dining room, round tables covered in starched white linens hosted dozens of different people who all looked very much alike. The women wore couture and the men sported handmade suits. A deep red carpet covered wood floors, drapes framed large floor-to-ceiling glass windows and an enormous crystal chandelier hung from the center of the room. Soft piano music played in the background, melding into the polite conversations, the clink of glasses and the subtle activities of the waitstaff.

The eastern wall of the room was glass, and gave a stunning view of the bay. Blue sky and clear water set off the sails of a dozen white sailboats. When he'd been in ICU, he'd promised himself that he would sail more when he recovered. And he had. He'd spent the last two weeks on the water. The boat had been yare and the weather stunning, but he'd found that sailing alone became tedious.

Alex headed to the large table in the back of the room. It was his grandmother's favorite table.

His grandmother had a Katharine Hepburn style that set her apart from her peers. Even at seventy-six her mind was sharp, and no one made a move at the club without her knowing it. He'd exhausted all conventional investigation methods after Kit had vanished. No tactic had revealed anything that cracked the case. Today, he thought he'd try a different approach.

Right after Kit's disappearance, Gertie had been in France, so he'd not questioned her, but now he realized she could give him a different perspective on the case.

Gertie's friends flanked her left and right. All wore suits in varying shades of red or blue, pearls around their necks and their white hair coiffed into tight curls.

Peering over turquoise reading glasses on her nose, Gertie frowned down at the cards in her hand. "Evelyn, I believe it's your turn to deal."

Evelyn, the woman to Gertie's right, leaned forward and took the pile of cards. "This time you are not going to win."

Gertie laughed. "We'll see."

Alex cleared his throat. "Gertie."

His grandmother glanced up and immediately smiled. "Alex, what a pleasant surprise! Ladies, you remember my grandson, *Detective* Alex Kirkland."

The emphasis on *detective* spoke to Gertie's support of his chosen profession. She was the only one in the family who'd approved of his decision.

Alex leaned down and kissed her on the cheek. "How are you?"

Pride glinted in her eyes. "Excellent. I am winning hand over fist today."

He smiled at the other ladies. "Watch out, ladies. She cheats."

The women laughed. Gertie appeared offended. "Alex, I know you didn't drive across town to question my card skills."

"Can't I just come to visit my grandmother?"

Gertie chuckled. "Darling, the club drives you insane. You come here only to get your boat. You never come in the main room and mingle."

Alex no longer felt as if he fit in here. He and the club members had less and less in common as the years passed.

He pulled up a seat and sat beside her. It felt good to have the weight off his leg. A waiter appeared and offered coffee, which he accepted.

"I'm looking into a case from last year. I was hoping you and your friends might be able to help."

Across the table, Evelyn dealt the next hand of gin rummy. "This sounds exciting. We'll help in any way we can."

The other women nodded.

Gertie removed her glasses. "We are all yours, my dear."

Alex loosened his tie. "Remember Kit Westgate?"

Each woman's face tightened, including Gertie's. "She's a hard woman to forget."

"What can you tell me about her?"

Gertie traced the rim of her half-full sherry glass with her fingertip. "West Coast money. Stunningly beautiful. Men could barely think straight when she was in the room. She had a way of making them fall under her spell just by the toss of her head or a smile."

Alex shifted, remembering his own reaction to Kit. "And?"

"I didn't like the woman," Gertie said. "I hate to speak ill of the dead, but she could be a cold-hearted manipulator. She could be quite unkind to Pierce. Granted he was a big boy and could take care of himself, but she had him completely wrapped around her finger and could make him do anything. It was rather sad to see."

That description contrasted what her chauffeur had told him last year. Borelli had described Pierce as abusive.

Evelyn picked up her cards and started to arrange them. "Remember the incident after the Founders' Ball last year?"

Gertie wrinkled her nose. "Kit got into a fight with the ladies' room attendant. She didn't realize I was in the last stall. Anyway, for a moment that cultured, smooth voice of hers slipped. For just a moment, she sounded very common. After that I never believed she was who she said she was."

"What were they arguing about?"

"Some woman named Brenda. I wasn't really paying attention."

"Pierce said he did a complete background check on her," Alex said. "In fact, he was quite helpful to the police, and supplied us with West Coast contacts."

"He did check her out completely," Gertie said. "He is a thorough man so he should know. And she did sign a prenup, so he was happy. According to the prenup, she wouldn't get a dime if she left him."

Across the table Roddie Talbot ran her finger along her neat strand of pearls. "Kit was quite chummy with her driver."

"Do you think they were having an affair?" Alex asked. The chauffeur had a record and had been a prime suspect until he'd produced ten witnesses who'd sworn he was in New York City.

"Who's to say if they were lovers?" Gertie said. "But I can tell you he was quite protective of Kit."

A clamor of noise had Alex lifting his head. He glanced toward the main entrance and saw a tall blond woman enter. She was wearing a Channel suit that matched her ice-blue eyes.

Regina. His ex-wife. Damn.

As if sensing Alex's presence, the blonde's gaze settled on him. Thin lips spread into a wide grin, and she brushed by the man she was with and hurried toward Alex, her arms open. "Alex!"

He had started dating Regina at Princeton, but they'd known of each other since preschool. Their union had thrilled his parents and been an anticipated step after college graduation. After he and Regina had married, Alex had dutifully attended law school, and Regina took her place in society, filling her days with committee meetings and lunches. Their marriage had been happy enough until Alex's cousin had died and Alex had chosen to join the police force. Regina had been furious. They'd fought bitterly. In the end, she'd asked him to choose between her and the career. He'd chosen the force.

Tension crept up Alex's spine as he rose. He hadn't seen Regina since just before the shooting, when she'd called him out of the blue. She'd just broken up with her latest boyfriend and he'd just solved the murder of a young boy. He'd allowed her to charm him and they had ended up in her bed. When he awoke the next morning, he knew he'd made a terrible mistake. She'd spoken of reconciliation. When he'd refused, she jetted off to Europe. Two days later, he was shot.

Two weeks ago she'd shown up at his home with a bottle of champagne and a gourmet meal made by her cook. She'd tried to rekindle their relationship again. This time he'd had the good sense to say no.

Regina's sweet perfume coiled around him as she kissed him on the cheek. "Alex, how are you?"

"Doing well."

"You look wonderful," she said, holding him at arm's distance and studying him. "Tell me you've given up any notion of returning to police work."

Nothing had really changed between them. "I started back today."

She pouted. "What a waste of good talent. I spoke to your brother Brandon the other day. He'd love to have you in the company."

Gertie drummed impatient manicured fingers on the table's white linen. "How goes plans for the Founders' Ball? It's less than a week away."

Regina brightened. She brushed an imaginary bit of lint from his shoulder, something she'd done a lot when they'd been married. "Excellent. We will transform this place tomorrow. It's a Monte Carlo theme this year."

"Wonderful," Gertie said.

His ex-wife missed the sarcasm in his grandmother's voice. The two had never gotten on well.

Alex decided to turn this meeting into an opportunity. "Regina, what do you remember about Kit Westgate?"

The blonde smiled. "Lovely woman. Such a sense of style. I would have killed for her skin."

"Anything unusual you remember about her?" Alex said.

"There was this one time when we were in New York shopping about eighteen months ago. We were on Fifth Avenue in Saks. Anyway, this shopgirl came up to Kit, hugged her and called her Brenda." Regina shuddered. "We were all shocked. Kit was furious. She told the woman that she was mistaken, and we left immediately."

Brenda. Gertie had heard Kit arguing about a woman named Brenda. "Could it have been a case of mistaken identity?"

Regina nodded. "That's what I thought. But it was strange. The woman was convinced that Kit was this Brenda."

"Anything else you remember about Kit?"

"No. Why are you asking? The woman has been dead for a year."

"I'm looking into the case. A loose end that's always troubled me."

Regina checked her diamond watch, caught sight of a male friend across the room and waved. "Honestly, Alex, why you would worry about an old case is beyond me. Kit is yesterday."

Understanding each other had been one of the major faults of their marriage. "Thanks, Regina."

She hooked her arm in his. "Walk me to my car?"

"Sure." Alex glanced at Gertie and her friends. They

shamelessly stared at the duo. None looked happy. "Ladies, thank you for your help." He kissed Gertie on the cheek. "Call me if you think of anything else."

"Of course, my dear," Gertie said.

Alex escorted Regina out of the club, aware that a half-dozen sets of eyes followed him. She was the darling of the club. He was the black sheep of his family and social set. No doubt everyone would be talking about him and his ex for days as whispers of reconciliation swirled. The club was like a small town where everyone knew everyone else's business.

When they came out on the portico, Alex spotted Tara's Toyota parked at the top of the circular drive. He glanced around, wondering where she lurked.

Regina tightened her hold on his arm. "Alex, darling, we really should get together again soon. It's been too long."

Regina was beautiful, and sex with her was always passionate if a bit lonely. It would be easy to fall into bed with her but he knew he'd be fooling himself and her if they did.

"Hey, sport!"

Tara Mackey's familiar voice caught Alex by surprise. He turned toward the east end of the building. A club security guard, who was an off-duty cop named Jimmy Rogers, was hauling Tara away from the club. She was trying to dig in her heels and pull against him, but resisting Jimmy was like trying to stop an avalanche. The guy was six-five and weighed close to two hundred and fifty pounds.

"You're gonna have to leave, ma'am," Jimmy said. His voice was calm. "This club is for members only."

"Let go of me, pal!" Tara shouted. "I told you I only need five minutes."

Jimmy kept pulling her toward the driveway. "No way."

A smile tipped the edge of Alex's lips. Regina was a beautiful woman, but compared to Tara she seemed spiritless and ordinary.

"Regina, if you will excuse me, I see a friend." He ignored her pout and headed toward Tara.

"Ma'am," Jimmy said. "You aren't allowed in the club."

"This is a free country. Free speech is in the Bill of Rights," Tara said. "I just want to talk to a few people."

The guard released Tara abruptly and she stumbled back. She barely caught herself before she fell on her backside.

Jimmy folded thick arms over his chest. "Leave or I call the cops."

"Look, man, I just want to talk to Mrs. Talbot. I promise I won't be a problem. I'll be in and out in five."

The guard reached into the breast pocket of his jacket and pulled out a cell phone. "I'm dialing the cops."

Tara's bravado faltered.

"Jimmy," Alex said, moving toward them. "What's the problem here?"

Jimmy's scowl softened. "Hey, Detective Kirkland. How you doing? No problem here. I was just about to have this reporter arrested for trespassing."

Tara glanced up at Alex. And for just a second her face colored as if she'd been caught with her hand in the cookie jar.

Alex took Tara's arm. "You don't have to worry about Ms. Mackey. I've got this under control."

Jimmy seemed grateful to be done with Tara. "Thanks, Detective."

Tara's expression turned glib. "Friends in high places, pal."

Jimmy shrugged and returned to his post back in the club.

Alex pulled Tara away. "Don't push your luck."

Tara followed until they were out of earshot and then jerked her arm free. "Thanks, Kirkland. I'm not sure where you came from but I appreciate the help. Now I have to figure out how to get into that club."

Her cheeks were flushed and her green eyes sharp with the prospect of a challenge. Her chest rose and fell rapidly, drawing his attention to her full breasts.

Alex realized he wanted to kiss her. *Damn.* Kiss Mackey. Where the hell had that come from? "Why do you want in the club?"

"I found Kit's old chauffeur but he didn't have much to add. So I figured I would visit the club—Kit Westgate's old hangout. I was hoping to ask around and see if anyone remembered her."

"No one's allowed in without a membership unless they are a guest of a member."

"Yeah, I know. But I thought maybe I could just slip in the side entrance. I was five feet in the side door when I was stopped by that goon. He said he spotted me because I don't blend in."

Alex studied her outfit. It didn't blend. Frankly, it was a shade too tight and sexy for the club. "You're just too…"

"Inexpensive, lowbrow, cheap?" The hint of defensiveness in her voice surprised him.

"Sexy."

She blushed. "*This* is not sexy."

That made him grin. "Come on, Mackey. You know how to work an outfit so that the male cops you interview don't think too clearly."

Mackey shrugged, unapologetic. "I get the quotes any way I can." She shot an annoyed glance back at the club.

"Get over it. You got caught and were tossed out."

She drew in a calming breath. "It's not that I mind getting caught. It's happened before. It's just that these highbrow types put me on the defensive. They think a big bankroll and a pedigree makes them better."

"Sounds like you've got issues." Tara Mackey was generally one of the most open-minded people he knew. "I'm surprised you have such a narrow view of the wealthy."

"You sound like Roxie."

"Roxie?"

"My aunt. She raised me."

The tidbit of information told him that he knew very little about Mackey personally. It was enough to make him curious about all the other things he didn't know about her.

Regina chose that moment to approach them. His ex looped her arm possessively around his. "Alex, who is your little friend?"

Her emphasis on *little* had Tara visibly bristly. She opened her mouth, ready to fire back an answer.

Alex cut Tara off before she could comment. "Regina, I'd like you to meet Tara Mackey. Tara is a crime reporter for the *Boston Globe*. Tara, this is Regina Albright."

Regina's brows rose. "A crime reporter? You must have met Alex at the police station."

Tara smiled, but he sensed her tension. "That's right."

Regina wrinkled her delicate nose. "Alex mentioned an article in the paper a few months ago. He wasn't pleased with the headline." She laid her manicured finger against her chin. "What was that headline? Oh, I remember. Arsonist Smokes Cops. That really made him mad."

Mackey's didn't flinch. "That was my piece. I was covering the north-side fires, set by an arsonist who called himself Nero."

Alex had called Mackey the day that article had come out. He had gotten her voice-mail and had expressed his displeasure in no uncertain terms. She'd responded later with a text message. *Glad u red my stuff*. "We caught the guy last week."

"And I reported that," Mackey added. "Brady had a few nice quotes as well."

Mackey's gaze dropped to Regina's hold on him. Her lips flattened. Some knew of his privileged background, but for the most part he downplayed it. He doubted Mackey knew. He could almost hear the wheels turning in her mind.

"Regina," Mackey said slowly. "How do you know Detective Kirkland?"

Regina grinned, looking like the cat that swallowed the canary. "Didn't Alex tell you about me?"

"No."

Alex pulled his arm free of Regina. "Regina and I were married a long, long time ago."

Chapter 4

Monday, July 14, 2:00 p.m.

Regina grinned. "Darling, it wasn't that long ago."

Tara's smile froze on her face. But mentally, her brain ticked through the facts she knew about the Albright family. Blue blood. Money. Privilege. They represented the worst possible combination as far as she was concerned. So what was a homicide cop like Kirkland doing mixed up with a family like that?

"I didn't realize that you'd been married." Tara's tone sounded extra cheery. She was trying to prove to Regina and herself that she didn't care that Kirkland had been married. It sure wasn't any of *her* business who he slept with or who he'd been married to.

Alex cleared his throat. "Regina and I have been divorced for eight years."

Regina pouted. "Has it been that long? It seems like it was only yesterday we were vacationing in St. Moritz for our honeymoon. And of course there was that cozy dinner at your house a few months ago."

Regina might as well have stamped *Mine* on Kirkland's forehead.

Again, Tara reminded herself that it was none of her business. "How'd you two hook up in the first place?"

Regina smiled. "We grew up together."

Albright. St. Moritz. Kirkland.

In a flash Tara connected the dots. How could she have been so stupid? The Kirkland family was the bluest of the blue bloods. His younger brother Brandon was constantly being quoted in the financial section. He was a wizard when it came to the financial markets. The family had more money than most small countries.

Alex *Kirkland* was not a regular guy a girl asked out for a beer or invited to a ballgame. "Kirkland, you're one of *the* Kirklands, aren't you?"

His jaw tightened. "Yes."

Regina laughed. "You didn't know? Good Lord, everyone knows Alex is the heir to the fortune."

Kirkland cleared his throat. "My brother runs the company. I'm a cop."

Tara suddenly felt foolish and awkward. She was a reporter. It was her job to know about people. But with Kirkland, she'd not looked past the badge and his reputation as a cop.

Again, she flashed the too-bright smile. "Hey, I'd love to stand here all day and chat. But I've got to go. Have a good one." She started across the circular drive toward her car.

"Mackey," Kirkland said.

She ignored him. It was unreasonable for her to be mad at him, but she was. She had really wanted him to be just a regular guy.

Kirkland caught up to her just as she reached her car. His grip on her arm was gentle but strong enough to stop her. "What's eating you?"

"Nothing."

"You're pissed that I slept with my ex a few months ago?"

"Please, I could care less about that."

His gaze narrowed. "So that means you have something against rich people."

Tara dropped her gaze to her purse and started to dig for her keys. Damn, where were they? "I've nothing against the rich."

"Look at me."

"No."

He laid his hand on her arm. "Coward."

She jerked her arm free, but continued to dig in her purse. Where were her keys? "Go away."

"Not until I explain."

She could feel the color rise in her face. "Explain what? You're rich. You have connections. Why you chose to downplay that fact is your business. It's not a big deal. Really."

He studied her face. "This is a big deal to you. Why?"

She refused to let this get to her. "What's a big deal is that I can't find my keys and I've got to get to work."

"At the paper?"

"At Roxie's bar. I wait tables there a few nights a week." Her fingertips brushed metal and she pulled out her keys. She jammed the key in the lock.

Kirkland shoved his hands in his pockets. "I downplay my background because I don't want it overshadowing my police work."

"You don't have to explain yourself to me." She opened the door.

He studied her closely. "Did some rich kid jilt you at one time?"

She got in the car and sat down. The last thing she wanted to do was examine her own prejudices, hang-ups and failed relationships. "Can we just drop it?"

He seemed to understand that she'd said all she

was going to say. Like a good interrogator, he changed tactics. "I talked to Regina about Kit."

That had her refocusing her attention back on him. "And?"

"Regina and Kit were in New York eighteen months ago and a saleswoman in Saks called Kit Brenda."

Curiosity ignited in her. "Did Regina know who the woman was?

"No. To her she was just a salesclerk." He shifted his stance as if his leg bothered him. "Kit told the woman she was mistaken and then demanded they leave the store."

Her mind ticked through the possibilities.

Kirkland's gaze narrowed. "I think you're right about there being more to this case. I'm going to move this case from the back burner to the front, Mackey."

Tara hid her smile. She hadn't thought he could leave the unsolved case alone for long. "And you will give me the scoop if you solve it before me?"

"Why should I?" A grin tipped the edge of his lips, and the smile changed his entire look. He wasn't classically handsome but there was a ruggedness—*a maleness*—that she found far more attractive.

"Because I'm the one that brought this case back to your attention and I've promised to share with you anything I find."

Amusement sparked in his eyes. "You share and I'll share?"

"It's a fair arrangement." She checked her watch. "Damn. Listen, I really do have to get going. I've got to stop by the paper before I get to Roxie's." She fired up the engine.

He stepped back from the car and she closed the door. "Be careful, Mackey. This case is going to ruffle feathers." He really looked worried.

"Ruffling feathers is what I do best. You know that." Gravel kicked up as she shoved the gear into Reverse and backed out of the parking lot, leaving Alex Kirkland staring after her.

The newspaper offices were busy when Tara arrived. She waved to the guard at reception and punched the up elevator button. The doors dinged opened to Bill Heckman, a tall, slim man with blond hair who always wore a Ramones T-shirt. This shirt was black with red lettering and a white skull. He was holding a stack of magazines and had an unlit cigarette behind his left ear.

Bill grinned. "Tara. How goes it?"

Tara and Bill had grown up in the same neighborhood. They had many friends in common from school and now both worked for the paper. They'd gone out a few times and Bill had wanted to get serious, but Tara had kept the relationship limited to friendship and the occasional Red Sox game. "It's going. Thanks again for that mock-up. It's been great."

"No sweat."

"Where you headed?"

"Going to the sports bar across the street. They're doing highlights of the Sox games from last year. Want to come?"

She was genuinely sorry she couldn't go. "I've got to work. Rain check?"

"Will do." He grinned. "Tell Roxie hi. And I'll be by on Saturday to fix that leaky faucet."

"Thanks, Bill." She kissed him on the cheek and got on the elevator. She punched Three and the doors closed. The elevator doors opened on the third floor to a large room with three rows of desks separated by narrow aisles. Most of the desks had reporters sitting at them. Everyone was either staring at a computer screen or talking on the phone. They were all racing to meet the evening deadline for the morning paper.

Tara hurried to her desk. Miriam had given her a week to work on the Westgate piece, so she had no evening deadline. The story was due in six days. She sat down and set her bag by her desk. She clicked on her computer.

While the machine booted up, she glanced at the stack of mail on her desk. Under the pile of various press releases and police incident reports she found a manila envelope. It had *T. Mackey* written on it. As she reached for it, her computer screen came on and she opened her e-mail. There were several Urgent Reply Requested e-mails from accounting regarding her last expense report. She dealt with those.

Her phone rang twice. She answered questions from two reporters before she got back to the envelope. She tore the sealed edge open.

Inside, she found a piece of paper folded crisply in half. She unfolded the paper and discovered it was a New York City rap sheet for a Brenda Latimer. Why on earth would someone send her Brenda Latimer's file? She checked the envelope for a note, but there was none.

Tara dropped her gaze to Brenda Latimer's picture. Immediately, the photo had Tara straightening. The girl was twenty-three or -four and had ink-black hair. A rebellious look glinted behind ice-blue eyes that were outlined in extremely heavy makeup.

There was no missing the similarities. The oval face, the graceful jawline and the high slash of cheekbones were unmistakable.

Brenda Latimer was a younger, less sophisticated version of Kit Westgate.

Chapter 5

Monday, July 14, 6:15 p.m.

As Tara drove through downtown traffic toward the turnpike, her head spun with possibilities. Had Kit Westgate Landover, last year's society darling, had a secret life before she came to Boston? This would change everything, and all the preconceived notions the police had regarding suspects would change.

The engine of Tara's car made a grinding sound as she shifted into a higher gear and got onto the turnpike.

Had Brenda become Kit? Or was this some hoax

designed to throw her off? She had no way of knowing until she did more digging.

Keep me posted. Kirkland's words echoed in her head. She had promised to keep him informed. And she would. Eventually.

For now, all she wanted to do was find out anything and everything on Brenda Latimer. She'd start with the police records in New York and work backward to Brenda's birth records, marriage records and any other bit of public information on file.

Tara reached into her purse and dug out her phone as she raced around a car. She dialed her aunt. Roxie picked up on the first ring and offered a raspy, "Hello."

"Roxie, it's me, Tara."

"Hey, kiddo."

"Can you survive without me at work for an hour or two this evening? I've got something I really have to do."

"Sure, doll, that's fine." She lowered her voice a notch. "Please tell me you have a date."

Tara smiled. Roxie had been after her for months to build some kind of social life outside of the paper and the bar. "I promise to give a full report when I get back."

"Good deal. Take care, sweetie."

"Thanks." She rang off, smiling. Tara had been six years old when her mother had died in a car crash. Roxie, her mother's sister, had just opened her bar and was an unlikely candidate for a guardian. When Tara's father had refused custody, Roxie hadn't hesitated, and had taken Tara into her life. Tara couldn't have asked for a better parent.

Tara tossed her cell on the passenger seat. Her mind turned back to work as she headed south on the turnpike. She'd just passed Fifth Street when she first noticed the black van in her rearview mirror. The driver was weaving in and out of traffic as if he was in a big hurry. He closed in on her quickly and came right up to her bumper.

"Okay, Mr. Jerk. What's the rush?" She gripped the steering wheel and switched lanes, figuring he wanted to pass her on the left. "That jerk's going to cause an accident," she muttered to herself.

She expected the van to pass, but instead he came up behind her and hovered right on her bumper. Gazing in the rearview mirror, she tried to get a look at the driver's face. Dark sunglasses and a oversize hood made it impossible to determine if the driver was a man or a woman.

She glanced to the passenger seat at her phone. She needed to call the cops. One hand tightly gripping the steering wheel, she leaned over to get her phone. The van was within inches of her bumper now.

When her fingers wrapped around the phone, she frantically flipped it open and dialed 9-1-1.

The van hit her bumper hard. Metal crunched

metal. Her car swerved. She screamed a few obscenities she'd learned from Roxie's patrons.

Tara dropped her phone and gripped the steering wheel with both hands. She righted the car and kept it on the road.

She expected the van to fall back, but instead it came toward her again. This time the driver hit her so hard she veered off the side of the road.

Her wheels crossed the white line of the shoulder and the next thing she knew she was skidding sideways. Her brakes squealed, and in one terrifying moment, her car flipped and her airbag deployed.

Alex hated hospitals. The antiseptic smells, the sound of gurneys passing and the hushed conversations all reminded him of the time he'd spent here, fighting for his own life. He'd come because Brady's oldest son, a rookie highway patrolman, had informed him that Mackey had been run off the road. Her car had been totaled and an ambulance had taken her to the hospital. Alex had left the office immediately and gone directly to St. Bridget's Hospital.

A day on his feet had taken a toll on his leg. His muscles had stiffened and his limp had returned. But there was nothing to be done about it as he moved down the hospital hallway toward the nurses' station. "I'm here for Tara Mackey."

The blond nurse peered over half glasses. She

looked tired, and her gaze was no-nonsense. "Are you family?"

"No." He reached into his breast pocket, pulled out his shield and flipped it open. "I'm with the Boston Police Department."

The nurse studied the badge carefully before nodding. "What can I do for you?"

Alex tucked the badge back in his pocket. "I'd like to see Ms. Mackey and talk to her about tonight's accident."

The woman's gaze brightened a fraction. "I can tell you that she's bruised and banged up, but she'll be fine."

"Thank God." Relief had him smiling. "Can I see her?"

"She's in cubical number five."

"Thanks."

"Detective, are you a friend of hers?"

He shoved his hand in his pocket. "You could say that."

"Good. Try to convince her to spend the night. She's bucking the doctors and trying to get herself released."

Arguing with doctors was pure Tara. "If her mind is set to leave, she'll be hard to sway. But I will try."

"Good luck."

He strode down the hallway and peeked around the curtain's edge to make sure he wasn't catching her in a delicate moment. Instead, he found Tara sitting in a chair by the exam table. Her hospital gown was on the floor, she'd put on her pants and she was trying to wrestle her shirt on. He caught a glimpse of her pink bra and the full swell of her breasts over the delicate lacy edge. He averted his gaze immediately, but had to admit he liked what he'd seen.

Kirkland took a step back. "Mackey, are you decent?"

"Kirkland?" She sounded surprised and a little embarrassed.

"Yep, it's me."

"Crap. What are you doing here?" It sounded as if she'd stepped away from the curtain.

"The responding officer was Brady's oldest son. He called me."

She groaned. "Do you know everyone in the Boston Police Department?"

Her feisty attitude told him she was going to be just fine. "Not everyone."

"Give me a second."

He heard the rustle of clothes. "Need any help?"

"No."

"Okay."

Seconds later she said, "I'm decent."

He pushed back the curtain and found her standing by the exam table dressed in the outfit she'd worn this morning in his office, except her shirt wasn't tucked in and her jacket lay on the chair. Her skin looked pale, and her hair hung loose just below her jawline.

He folded his arms over his chest. "The nurse wants you to spend the night."

She rolled her eyes. "She's just being overly cautious. The doctor said I could leave if I really wanted to."

He didn't like her coloring or the bruise forming on her collarbone. "What's the rush, Mackey? Spend the night."

She ran her hands through her hair. "No thanks. I'll be better off at home in my own bed."

He liked the way her thick and lush hair swung loose around her jawline. He wondered if it was as soft as it looked. "You should take it easy in a hospital bed for a night."

"No. I've got to get home."

"Why? Someone waiting on you?" It occurred to him that it could be a boyfriend waiting. And that didn't sit well with him.

"As a matter of fact someone is waiting for me."

Alex had never felt the sting of jealousy, but now for some reason he did. "Who?"

Wincing, she reached for her purse on the chair. "Why do you care?"

"It wouldn't be wise for you to be home alone."

She started to dig into her purse. "I'm not going to be alone."

"Good."

Mackey found her cell phone and flipped it open. "I know Brady Junior called you, but what are you doing here, Kirkland?"

He was here because he'd needed to see for himself that she was okay. The protective urge didn't make sense, but it had overridden all logic. "I heard you were giving the nurses hell."

She blushed. "If they'd just listen to me, I wouldn't be so difficult."

He rested his hands on his hips. "You were run off the road by a car on the turnpike. They had reason to be concerned."

She started to dial a number and then stopped. "But I didn't lose one hundred IQ points in the process. They are treating me like a baby."

He understood the feeling. When he'd started to mend from the gunshot wound, the constant monitoring of nurses and doctors had driven him crazy. Mackey was wired like he was, and he knew there was no sense arguing the point. "Tell me about the accident."

She closed the phone and drew in a breath. He could tell recalling the incident made her uncomfortable. "A van came out of nowhere and got right on my bumper. I moved to the right lane but he followed. Then he hit my bumper with his. I ran off the road."

That bothered him. She could easily have been killed

or badly injured. "Was it a road-rage incident? Did you cut in front of someone while you were driving?"

Her gaze narrowed. "That's what the other cop asked."

Lifting a brow, he waited for her answer.

Glaring at him, she started to tuck her shirt in, but winced as if her shoulder hurt. "No, I didn't cut in front of someone. I was minding my own business when the black van found me."

Alex tried to distance himself emotionally so he could focus on the facts. He wasn't having much luck. "Did you get a look at the driver?"

She ran her fingers through her hair, pulled a rubber band from her pocket and tied her hair back. "No. Sunglasses and a hood covered his face."

He tightened his jaw and released it. "Where were you headed?"

She hesitated a second. "South. To Roxie's."

Despite his effort to remain emotionally neutral, he was very worried about her. "When you went off the road, did the driver approach you?"

She frowned at the memory and swayed a fraction. "No. Thank God. I was really rattled."

He took ahold of her arm and guided her to the chair by the exam table. "You should be sitting down."

She pressed her fingertips to her temple. "I'm fine," she said, setting her jaw. "Some jerk on the highway is not going to interfere with my life. He's already screwed up my evening. I'm going home." She rose, gingerly set her purse on the exam table and scanned the room with her gaze. "Do you see my shoes anywhere?"

He spotted the flats under the bed, picked them up but held on to them.

She smiled weakly as she slipped on the shoes. "Now all I need is a cab and I'll be set. I need to get home so my aunt doesn't start worrying."

The bit of information pleased him. "*Your aunt* is waiting on you?"

"Yes." She reopened her cell. "I live on the top floor of the building she owns. She has the second floor, and her bar, Roxie's, is on the first floor."

"Right." He knew next to nothing about her personal life but found he wanted to know more. "Does she know that you're here?"

Mackey looked a bit embarrassed. "No. And I want to keep it that way. She will freak out if she knows what happened. Her sister—my mother—died in a car accident. She's the reason I can't spend the night at the hospital. If I do, she will know something is wrong."

He grinned. "I always figured you were a free spirit. Not the kind that lives with an aunt."

She shrugged. "My aunt is getting older. She needs help with the bar. Living on-site saves me money and helps her out. Do you have the number of the Ace cab company? I can't seem to remember it now."

"You're not taking a cab. I'll give you a ride home. Just stay put while I get your discharge papers."

She looked genuinely relieved. "Thanks, Kirkland. I owe you."

Kirkland spent the next twenty minutes convincing a Dr. Finley that Mackey was leaving. The doctor wasn't as ready for her to leave as Mackey had said, but finally, with assurances from Kirkland that she'd rest, the doctor relented.

Forty-five minutes later, a nurse pushed Mackey's wheelchair to the patient pickup while Alex retrieved his Impala. He came around to the passenger side of the car and helped her out of the wheelchair. Gingerly, she lowered into the seat. He could see she was hurting.

She started grinning, as if she'd been told a joke.

He leaned inside the open door. "What's so funny?"

Tara shifted in the seat until she was comfortable. "I've got bruised ribs. You've got a limp. We make one hell of a pair."

Alex frowned. "I don't have a limp anymore."

She glanced up at him. "It was barely noticeable this morning. But now that you're tired it's more pronounced. Face it, we are the walking wounded."

Alex didn't respond, and closed her door. As he walked around the car he made an effort not to limp. The bit of showmanship cost him. His leg really ached when he got in the car.

Mackey raised a brow. "Nice show. You almost hid it completely that time."

"I don't have a limp." He fired up the engine.

A flash of pain crossed her face as she clicked her seat belt buckle into the lock.

"It was a mistake to pull you out of the hospital. I can see you're hurting."

She breathed out a long breath and met his gaze head on. "Hey, if you don't have a limp then I don't have bruised ribs."

He couldn't help but grin. "You are a real pain, Mackey."

She laid her head back against the seat, exposing the long curve of her neck. "Tell me something I don't know."

He wondered if her skin was as soft as it looked. "So where to?"

She gave him the address. It was a working-class neighborhood twenty minutes away from the hospital. They drove in silence. She closed her eyes and drifted off to sleep.

He glanced at her a couple of times. Sleeping, she looked different. Young. Vulnerable. He'd learned more about Tara Mackey today than he'd learned in the past year.

When he pulled onto her block, the streets were quiet, and he had no trouble finding a parking spot in front of the brick building. He shut off the car engine.

On the bottom floor of the building in a large window, a pink neon Roxie's sign was flickering. A Closed sign hung in the door. The place looked like any other neighborhood bar. He imagined it came with its own cast of regulars.

He glanced at Mackey, trying to imagine her growing up here. His own childhood had been privileged and he'd not had to work. Everything had been taken care of.

"Mackey," he said softly. "We're here."

Her head snapped up. She ran tense fingers over her hair. The bar was quiet, but the second-floor light was on. "Hey, would you do me a favor?"

"Need help getting out of the car?"

She smoothed the wrinkles from her shirt as she glanced at the second-floor window. "That, too."

He lifted a brow. "What else?"

"Pretend to be my date?"

That was the last thing he'd expected her to say. "Say that again."

"When the ambulance driver told me I had to go to the hospital, I called my aunt and told her that I couldn't make it in to work at the bar tonight because I had a date. I don't want her knowing I was in the hospital. She worries."

He shifted his arm over the seat behind her and turned toward her. Moonlight accentuated the high slash of her cheekbones. "Your aunt is okay with you missing work for a date?"

A wry smile tipped the edge of her lips. "She'd sell her soul if she knew I was dating. Her fondest dream is that I marry and give her grandnieces and grand-nephews." She blushed as if she'd not meant to be so direct. "Just show your face, and I'll make up a quick story and you can be on your way. You can pretend you like me for a couple of minutes, can't you?"

He'd have no trouble pretending with Mackey. "Sure."

Chapter 6

Tuesday, July 15, 12:01 a.m.

Tara had chosen the lesser of two evils. To avoid telling her overprotective aunt that she'd nearly been killed in a car accident, she'd asked Kirkland for a personal favor.

Now Tara wasn't so sure she'd made the right choice.

Normally, she wouldn't have asked him for anything. She didn't like owing the cops she covered, and for some reason she especially didn't want to be beholden to Kirkland. He was sharp—one of the best detectives she'd ever met. He worked hard and didn't expect any more from the people under him than he was willing to give himself. Because she respected him so much, she'd always made sure she'd done her homework when she was around him.

Add in the fact that he was one of the social elite, and she felt really uncomfortable bringing him into her world. The last time she'd brought one of his kind into her life it had met with disastrous consequences.

She was not ashamed of her family or her roots. She adored Roxie. But her aunt's outspoken opinions and colorful language could make even the toughest longshoremen blush. She flashed back to her thirteenth birthday, when Roxie had arrived at her party dressed in a pink muu-muu, a sparkly hat, crooning "Happy Birthday" in her whiskey voice. Tara had been mortified.

Kirkland pocketed his keys and came around the car. This time the pain in her shoulder had her waiting for him to open her door. Cool night air rushed over her as he held his hand out to her.

She accepted it and carefully rose. "Thanks."

The look in his eyes was tender. "No problem."

Evening shadows accentuated the lines creasing the corners of his eyes. His brown hair was brushed back, emphasizing his angular face and stark blue eyes. Even knowing his background, she couldn't picture him lounging on a yacht or whiling away the afternoon at the country club golf course. He was the kind of guy who needed to be in the center of the action.

Tara pushed aside the thoughts. She was not going to get involved with this guy.

"Brace yourself," Tara warned. "My aunt Roxie is quite the character.

Kirkland pressed his hand into the small of her back, steadying her as she fumbled with her keys. "She can't be that bad."

"She's just going to be very excited. It's been a little too long since she's seen me date. She's going to be all over you."

"You worry too much."

She shot him an I-warned-you look and pushed open the heavy wooden door. Bells jingled over her head.

Mondays were slow nights, and the place had all but cleared out by eleven. The faint smell of beer and cigarettes permeated the large room filled with chairs turned upside down on round tables. The floors had been freshly mopped and the large wooden bar wiped clean.

The quiet stillness was enough to let Tara hope that Roxie had gone to bed, which would have been a minor miracle. But she'd not taken two steps when the swinging door behind the bar pushed open.

Roxie wore her big blond hair teased high, blue eye shadow and a T-shirt that accentuated double-D breasts. She sported silk pajama pants and fuzzy slippers. The woman grinned broadly when she saw Tara and Kirkland.

"Roxie," Tara said. "I thought you'd have called it a night by now."

"Me? No way, not with my baby girl out on a date." Roxie boldly stared at Kirkland. "Well, it's about time you two lovebirds got back."

Roxie crossed the distance between them and hugged Tara, who did her best not to cringe as her aunt squeezed her bruised shoulder.

"So, who is your friend?" Again, Roxie boldly stared at Kirkland as though he were a fresh slab of meat.

Kirkland didn't bat an eye.

"Roxie, this is Detective Alex Kirkland." Tara cleared her throat. "He's my date this evening."

Kirkland put out his hand. "Nice to meet you, Ms. Mackey."

Roxie moistened her lips and in a deep, throaty voice said, "You call me Roxie." She winked approvingly at Tara. "You could have knocked me over with a feather when Tara told me she had a date. The kid works all the time. Too hard, if you ask me. It's about time she had some fun."

"Roxie," Tara warned.

"What? You do work too hard. And you don't have any fun." She shifted her gaze to Alex. "During the day it's the paper and in the evening she's here slinging drinks. There have even been times, like when she was working on those vagrant murders, that she would write all night after her shift here. She makes me tired just looking at her."

Alex glanced at Tara. "I didn't realize it was such a push to write those articles."

Tara shrugged, refusing to admit it had stretched her to the limit to get them done. "It really was no big deal."

Their exchange went over Roxie's head. Her focus was on Kirkland. "Very, very nice, Tara. So where did Mr. Handsome take you tonight?"

Tara fumbled to come up with a story.

Kirkland smiled. "Dinner, and then we drove around."

"Where'd you eat?" Roxie asked Kirkland.

"Roxie," Tara warned. "No third degree."

Roxie shrugged. "When you called and said you were on a date, I told you I wanted details. So where'd you eat?"

"Brenan's," Kirkland supplied.

Roxie nodded approvingly. "Very nice. So where did you and my Tara meet?"

"She covers the crime beat," Kirkland said. "I'm a cop. We've crossed paths regularly."

Roxie lifted a penciled-on brow. "So, Detective Alex Kirkland, what kind of policeman are you? Not vice, I hope."

His laugh sounded genuine and relaxed. "Homicide."

Roxie's eyes widened with approval. "Very nice. Detective, can you stay for a cup of coffee?"

Experience had taught Tara that the best lies were the least complicated ones, and the sooner she got Kirkland out of here the better. "Roxie, he has an early-morning roll call."

Kirkland shook his head. "A cup of coffee won't hurt."

Tara tried not to groan.

Roxie winked at him. "Come on over to the bar. I just made a fresh pot."

Tara's shoulder ached and she braced herself to climb up on a bar stool. Kirkland surprised her by pulling out a stool and helping her up in such a way that the gesture looked more loving than helpful. His touch was solid and steady and made her heart race a little faster. He took a seat beside her.

Roxie went around to the bar and set two mugs in front of Kirkland and Tara. She filled each with coffee. "So it's taken a year for you two to finally go out on a date."

Kirkland thanked her for the coffee. "We both lead busy lives."

Roxie wasn't convinced as her gaze skipped between the two. "So what did you learn about my baby tonight?"

"Not much," Kirkland said. "She plays her cards close."

"That's my girl." Roxie leaned forward and rested her chin on her hand. "What do you want to know about Tara?"

Tara set her coffee mug down. A bit of coffee sloshed onto her hand. "Roxie, that's enough. Kirkland doesn't want to hear about my boring past."

Roxie shrugged. "Baby, you are not boring."

A teasing light sparked in Alex's eyes. "Your niece didn't say much about herself. She's very tight-lipped and very guarded."

Roxie nodded. "That's my T. Has been like that since she was a kid."

Tara's gaze narrowed. If she could have run from the room she would have. "I'm not that interesting."

Roxie waved her away. "She's very modest. She is brilliant. I have a scrapbook full of her articles from the *Post* and the *Globe*. My baby is going to win a Pulitzer one day. The scrapbook is in the back. I can get it if you want to see it."

Tara pushed off her stool, wincing as her feet hit the ground. "Roxie, no—really. Alex really does have an early call in the morning."

Kirkland slid off the stool and stood beside her. This close, she realized how much he towered over her. "Tara's right. I do have an early-morning call."

Roxie nodded. "Hey, I understand how hard you boys in blue work. As far as I'm concerned they don't pay you guys enough. So remember, there's always a free beer or coffee waiting for you at Roxie's."

Kirkland's smile was genuine. "Thanks."

"Will you be seeing my girl again?"

Before Tara could come up with some excuse, Kirkland said, "I hope so."

Roxie winked. "Good. Because I like you, Detective Kirkland. Tara, go ahead and escort your date out to his car. That is the polite thing to do."

Tara was grateful to be making an exit. "Absolutely." She walked Kirkland to the curb. "Thanks again. I really appreciate the ride home, and you speaking to Roxie. She can be a little bold."

He smiled. "She seems like a good person."

"She is. And I love her to death. But there are times when I cringe."

He kept his gaze on her and, lowering his voice, said, "You know she's staring at us."

"Did I mention she's overprotective? It's just the two of us, and she worries." Energy and heat radiated from his body. She had to concentrate to not stare at his full lips.

Alex leaned forward. "I think she's waiting for me to kiss you."

Her mouth went dry. "What?"

"You've heard of a kiss, haven't you, Mackey? It's when…"

She glanced into the bar and saw Roxie boldly

staring at them. Roxie grinned and waved. "I know what a kiss is, Kirkland. And don't worry about it. You've gone above and beyond the call of duty today."

He slid his hand around the back of her neck. "I'd hate to disappoint Roxie. And if we're pretending we're on a date we might as well put on a good show."

Before she could protest, he leaned his face forward and pressed his lips to hers. The kiss was light, soft, but it stirred a heat inside her she hadn't experienced in a very long time.

He pulled back a few inches but he was still close enough that his warm breath brushed her face. "You think that is enough to convince Roxie?"

Her heart hammered against her ribs. It wasn't enough for her. "Yes."

A slight smile tipped the edge of his mouth. "Maybe one more, just for good measure."

She moistened her lips. "Oh, that's not necessary."

"Better to be thorough."

"Okay."

The second kiss wasn't so chaste, and he lingered longer. She tipped her head to the side as his tongue teased her lips open for him. His tongue caressed the inside of her mouth.

Tara wrapped her arm around his neck and forgot about Roxie, the article, even Kirkland's pedigree. There was only this kiss. This very incredible kiss.

When he pulled away, his eyes burned with a

desire that made her knees weak. He dropped his hand to her shoulder. He, too, seemed as surprised by the intense desire as she had been.

She was reluctant to step back, but she did. "Thanks. I really do owe you for everything."

A faint smile tipped the edges of his mouth as he pushed a stray strand of hair back into place. "You don't owe me a thing. The pleasure was mine." He turned back to the bar and waved to Roxie, who gave him a thumbs-up, and then got in his car and drove off. Tara went back into the bar.

Roxie nodded approvingly at her. "Now, him I approve of."

Tara held up her hand. "No more questions."

Roxie lifted a brow. "What? Me? Hey, far be it from me to stick my nose into your personal life. But he seems very nice. A keeper."

"He's a good man." That was as much as she was willing to admit. She didn't dare voice the feeling she'd felt when he'd kissed her.

Roxie refreshed Tara's coffee. "So, now that it's just us girls, tell me what's really going on."

Tara eased up on the stool. "What do you mean?" Her aunt could spot a lie twenty miles off.

"Oh, he's a good-looking fellow, and I'd like to see you two hook up, but you two weren't on a date."

Tara felt as if she were seven and had just gotten caught egging the neighbor's house. "What?"

Roxie tucked a bleached curl behind her ear. "Doll, I wasn't born yesterday. Spill. Where is your car, and what happened to your shoulder?"

Chapter 7

Tuesday, July 15, 1:20 a.m.

Roxie spent the next hour squeezing every detail out of Tara regarding the accident. The more Tara talked the more worried Roxie looked.

"I swear on your mother's grave, Tara, you better be more careful or I'm going to lock you in your room."

Tara grinned. "I'll be fine. Don't worry."

Roxie leaned forward, her gaze hard and direct. "Don't be afraid? You were run off the road."

The details of the accident had already started to get hazy. "It could have been just a dumb accident."

"Honey, if you've been stirring up questions about Kit Landover, I don't think it was any kind of mishap. I know from personal experience that Pierce Landover doesn't always play by the rules."

That surprised Tara. "How do you know Pierce Landover?"

Roxie shrugged and glanced down at her red, manicured fingernails. "I know a lot of people."

Tara knew her aunt had lived a full life before she'd adopted her. But once Tara had come to live with her, Roxie had settled down quite a bit. She'd been dating the same guy, Tommy Sloan, a foreman on the docks, for twelve years. "It's your turn to spill."

Roxie studied her long red nails. "We crossed paths back in the old days." She twirled a bleached blond lock with her fingers.

"Were you and Pierce—" Tara struggled to find the right word "—intimate."

Roxie shrugged, unapologetic. "Yeah, if that's what you want to call it. We saw each other before he married his first wife, Grace, and then a few more times after they divorced. Pierce might have married into one of Boston's first families, but he liked his women a little rougher around the edges."

Tara sat back, blinked. "Roxie, I am amazed."

"What do you want to know about Pierce?"

"Do you think Landover is the kind of guy that could kill his wife?"

"Hard to say. He does have a temper. And he expected his women to stay in line." She grinned. "That's why we didn't work out. I didn't like being bossed around."

Tara was stunned. "Wow."

Roxie frowned. "I can tell you that Pierce likes his private life to stay private. Image is very important to him. So be careful."

"That's what Kirkland said."

"Smart man." Roxie grinned. "I'll try to be more subtle when you bring Alex around again."

Tara suddenly felt uneasy. "What makes you think I'm going to be bringing him around again?"

"Oh, honey, if Roxie knows anything, it's sexual chemistry, and you two definitely have that."

Tara woke with a terrible headache and a sore shoulder. Her ribs also ached. She gently swung her legs over the side of the bed and eased her bare feet onto the blue shag carpet by her bed. Rising, she moved into the main room of her apartment, which was located on the third floor of Roxie's building.

Her apartment was a small space, only eight hundred square feet, and everything in the place served double duty. Shelves lined the walls and held hundreds of books, knickknacks and art covered most of the walls. Storage chests doubled as end tables, and the few real pieces of furniture she had were on casters so she could move them around to suit her needs. She liked the small space because it forced her constantly to edit the possessions in her life.

She elected to skip her morning run and savor a second cup of coffee before showering and dressing in loose-fitting pants and a cotton top. She spent the next hour on the phone with the insurance company. The car was covered and the company would give her a rental car for two weeks. A few more calls and she found a company that fit into their budget.

Tara opened the file on the Westgate article but found it difficult to concentrate. Her mind kept wandering to Kirkland. She'd had her eye on the guy since she'd started freelancing in the city a year ago. She'd been doing a piece on gang violence, and when she'd gotten a tip that there'd been a shooting, she'd gone to the scene. That was the first time she'd seen Kirkland. She'd tried to interview him but he'd barely given her the time of day. His arrogance had made her angry. In fact, she'd shared a few choice words with him when he'd ordered the patrolmen to keep her behind the yellow tape.

Then she'd watched as he'd methodically analyzed the crime scene. He'd spotted things the forensic techs had missed. He'd spoken so gently to the victim's grieving mother. She'd known then that Kirkland could be a hard-ass, but he was a class act.

Tara shoved out a breath. "Don't go down this path. He's got wrong-guy-for-you written all over him."

She sipped her coffee and refocused on her notes. Her career was the most important thing in her life.

It had been warm the night Kit had vanished. She'd been wearing a designer wedding dress made of white satin with a thousand cultured pearls hand-sewn on the bodice and hem of the dress. A year-old news account reported that the necklace, earrings and bracelet were family heirlooms and had been in the Landover family for six generations. The article quoted a local jeweler, Frederick Robinson, who said the pieces were valued conservatively at fifteen million dollars. Even the pearls on her dress had been worth over one hundred thousand dollars.

The estate's greenhouse had been soaked in the socialite's blood, but her body was never found. Kit's dress was discovered by the river one week later, but the pearls sewn into it and the diamonds had never surfaced.

Tara glanced at Brenda's mug shot. She picked up the phone and called a colleague at the newspaper, who gave her a contact in the New York Police Department. A few phone calls later and she'd gotten ahold of a woman in the records department who had promised to do some digging for her.

She then called a friend of hers who was a male nurse at Boston General. It took a few minutes for her call to get transferred, but finally she heard a familiar, "Tara."

"David, how are you doing?" She'd known David since college. Her friend wore his ink-black hair short, and he generally dressed in jeans and flannel shirts. He was a talented surgical nurse who also taught at the university. And David saw conspiracy theories everywhere. His was the perfect brain to pick about Kit's disappearance.

"Good!" David said. "I haven't talked to you in months."

"Sorry about that. Work has been insane."

His deep voice dropped a notch. "When are we going to catch another concert?"

She hoped David had figured out that friendship was all Tara could give. "Name the time, and I'll be there."

"As a matter of fact, I've two tickets to a jazz festival in two weeks."

"Count me in."

"I'm going to hold you to that one. So, what can I do for you?"

"I'm working on an article about an unsolved case." She ran down the details of Kit's story. "So is there any way someone could survive losing five pints of blood?"

"No. Not a chance. That's over half the body's blood volume. Brain function would cease."

Her shoulders slumped. "Are you sure?"

"Very."

Tara sighed. "That shoots down my theory. I had this half-baked idea that somehow Kit survived all that blood loss."

"Ah, a conspiracy theory. Now you're talking my language. Give me a second to think." After a moment's pause he said, "Actually, the blood thing wouldn't be hard to fake."

Tara sat straighter. "The blood was Kit's. DNA was a perfect match."

"I've no doubt the blood was hers. But, what if she started banking her blood months before she vanished?"

"It would keep that long?"

"Sure, as long as it was frozen. All she'd need is access to a freezer."

"Wow, I hadn't thought about that. Outlandish."

"But possible." David sounded pleased with himself.

"Hey, thanks. You've earned yourself a steak dinner."

"Excellent. You can feed me before the concert."

"Done."

Tara hung up the phone. It was a crazy theory, but not an impossible one.

Five minutes later the phone rang. The woman on the other end from the New York Police Department's records office gave Tara Brenda Latimer's basic stats, including her year and place of birth and the list of charges.

Excited, Tara thanked the woman and hung up.

Brenda and Kit's birth years matched. And one of the charges leveled against Brenda had been fraud.

For the sake of argument, Tara decided to assume that Brenda had created Kit and that she had vanished with the gems intentionally on her wedding day.

If Kit/Brenda had done all that, she'd have to have found a buyer for the jewels. The likely place to start was the jeweler who had appraised the gems, Frederick Robinson. He could give Tara a full description of what went missing so that she knew what to look for. He could also help her figure out how such unusual pieces could be fenced.

After she spoke with Robinson's Jewelers, she'd track down more details about Brenda.

Two hours later, Tara had taken a cab to the rental-car place and driven to the area where the ritzy Beacon Hill jeweler was located. She'd dressed in a black pantsuit and pulled her hair back in her customary tight ponytail. She'd chosen patent-leather flats and a costume pearl brooch she'd bought at a flea market years ago.

Tara followed her directions to the letter but the jewelry store was harder to find than she'd first thought. It didn't have display windows filled with gems or even obvious signage. There was simply the street number above the door and a small sign that read Robinson's.

She parked across the street and walked toward the shop, only to discover the front door was locked.

And there were surveillance cameras trained on the spot where she stood.

She rang the bell by the front door.

After a two- or three-second delay the door buzzed and the lock opened. She went into the shop.

Sitting behind a large oak desk was a small man with gray hair, a neatly trimmed goatee and rectangular reading glasses. He wore a tweed suit, a crisp white shirt and a red tie. A rich oriental rug warmed the floor and the walls were exposed brick. Large gilded mirrors hung on each wall. No gems were displayed. She had the sense she'd walked into a banker's or lawyer's office.

The jewelry stores she was accustomed to were the kind found in a mall. They had large display cases, large Sale signs and a half-dozen hungry salespeople looking to make a monthly quota off the walk-in customers.

The man rose. "Mrs. Freedman?"

"Uh, yes." He didn't look like the kind of guy who would talk to reporters.

He moved around the desk with an economy of motion. "Welcome to Robinson's. I am Frederick Robinson. I wasn't sure if you were going to make our appointment."

"I'm sorry. Traffic. There was a pileup in town, *again*." She didn't know who Mrs. Freedman was but decided to run with it.

Mr. Robinson held out his hand to a plush chair in front of his desk. “Would you like to have a seat?”

She smiled, praying Mrs. Freedman was running very, very late. “Lovely.”

“Coffee? I have your favorite brand brewing. St Helena?”

“You are so clever, Mr. Robinson.”

He smiled, pleased with his attention to detail as he moved through a door into a back room. Minutes later he appeared with a silver tray holding a steaming cup of coffee in a lovely antique cup on a matching saucer, along with a plate of sugar cookies.

She accepted the cup and sipped the coffee. “Delicious.”

“I understand you are interested in a necklace.”

“Yes.”

He turned to the paneled wall behind him and pressed it. The panel popped open and behind it stood a huge safe. Mr. Robinson blocked her view with his body as he twisted the large bronze dial several times. The lock clicked open. The massive door swung open. He removed a long, slim velvet box, set it on his desk and opened the lid. Blinking up at her were twelve of the largest diamonds she’d every seen.

The cup in her hand rattled and she gingerly set it on the table. She’d never seen such beautiful jewelry. “They are stunning.”

"You said on the phone that you were looking for large, unique pieces. Preferably yellow diamonds."

She leaned forward and looked at the stones. "Yes. I'm thinking about having a necklace made."

"We can certainly accommodate you."

Tara pictured the photo of Kit's necklace. The center stone had been a ten-carat pink diamond. "These are wonderful, but I've changed my mind about the color."

"What were you looking for?"

"Now, don't laugh."

He flattened his thin lips. "Never."

"I have always envied the piece Kit Westgate Landover wore on her wedding day. She also wore it in the engagement photo that the press ran again and again after she vanished."

He tugged the edge of his cuff. "That was a tragic event."

"Tragic." She hesitated for effect. "And such a lovely woman."

A subtle tension settled in his shoulders. "Yes, she was a beauty." His body language suggested Kit was also difficult. "She insisted on the best."

Tara leaned forward. "I was at the Founders' Yacht Club yesterday and was speaking with Regina Albright. By the way, when I mentioned I was coming here, she spoke highly of your work."

He beamed. "Excellent."

"We were talking about what a waste it was to lose so many lovely diamonds. Did those gems ever surface?"

He leaned toward her. "No. But I will tell you Mr. Landover insisted the family diamonds be engraved with a laser. Not visible to the naked eye, mind you, but under a high-powered microscope, the three largest diamonds have the letter *L* on them."

"So if anyone tried to sell the diamonds..." she let the statement trail.

"They'd have to be authenticated, and the mark would be discovered. The police department put out a notice to all jewelers that the gems were connected to a murder."

"But what if it were sold to a private collector?"

"Few jewelers broker gems that large. In general we are a small community, and word gets around."

"But you know of such jewelers?"

"Of course."

The front doorbell buzzed and Tara grabbed her purse. No doubt the real Mrs. Freedman had arrived.

Mr. Robinson looked at the monitor behind his desk. He frowned. "Now that's unusual."

She rose, glancing around to see if there was a back door. There wasn't.

He buzzed the door open. "Sorry for this interruption, Mrs. Freedman."

Damn. "No trouble at all."

Mr. Robinson came around the desk, his spine as stiff as a plank. "Detective Kirkland."

"Mr. Robinson." Kirkland's smooth voice sent tingles up Tara's spine. Double damn.

"I am currently with a client, Detective," Mr. Robinson said.

"This won't take a minute," Kirkland said.

Tara was stuck. There was no getting out of this jam. So she turned and smiled brightly at Kirkland.

Surprise flickered in Kirkland's ice-blue eyes for only an instant before he flashed even white teeth. "I believe we have met before."

Tara raised her chin. "Have we?"

Mr. Robinson cleared his throat. "Detective, this is Mrs. Eloise Freedman."

Kirkland shook his head. "Actually, Mr. Robinson, this is Tara Mackey. She's a reporter for the *Globe*."

Tara let out a sigh. Leave it to Kirkland to be the Boy Scout.

Robinson grimaced with disgust. "You lied to me."

Tara shrugged. "You made the assumption I was Mrs. Freedman. I played along."

Robinson frowned. "I must ask you to leave my store immediately, Ms. Mackey."

"I just have a few questions about the Landover diamonds."

Mr. Robinson moved toward the door and opened

it. "Ms. Mackey, we do not speak to the press. Robinson's has a very elite clientele and most do not want the publicity."

"You were happy to gossip about the Landovers before."

Robinson's face turned red. "That's when I thought you were one of us."

One of us. Again, she was on the outside looking in. She glanced at Kirkland. "Come on, tell Mr. Robinson that I'm okay. If someone says off the record, I honor it."

Kirkland shook his head. "I can vouch for that, Mr. Robinson."

"Ms. Mackey, I don't talk to any press. Period," Robinson said. "Leave, or I will have the detective call a squad car."

She shot Kirkland a glare.

He shrugged. "This is a job for the police, not the press."

She stepped out onto the curb and Robinson closed the door in her face.

Alex had to give Tara credit. The woman had nerve. He wasn't sure how she'd wormed her way into the exclusive shop, but somehow she'd managed it. He pulled out his notebook. This investigation wasn't a game.

Robinson straightened his tie. "I am sorry about

that. I assumed her name was Freedman because the real Mrs. Freedman had an appointment."

"Don't feel too bad. She's a smart reporter. You're not the first one she's fooled." He flipped through the pages of his notebook. "I have a few questions about Kit Landover."

He sighed, as if already weary about the topic. "I'll tell you what I told that woman. The diamonds have not surfaced."

"None of your sources have gotten back to you? Including the less-than-reputable ones?"

"None."

Kirkland met the jeweler's gaze. "You wouldn't hold back on me, would you Mr. Robinson? I'd hate for it to get out that you did time for fencing."

Mr. Robinson cleared his throat. "That was a long time ago and you know it. I've been clean for ten years."

"Come on, Lenny," Kirkland said, using Robinson's real name. "This business was built on profits from your former crimes. A diamond like the Landover one would be a very sweet coup. They could make a guy like you very rich."

The jeweler dropped the pretense of a refined jeweler. "Look," he said in a rougher voice. "I ain't seen the diamonds. And, like I told that reporter, the stones were marked and are easy too track. Too much trouble to handle even for me."

"Who else knew the diamonds were marked?"

"We have been through all this a year ago." Robinson reached into his pocket, pulled out a cigarette and lit it. "Just Landover knew about the marks."

"And you."

"I marked 'em."

"Did Kit know?"

"Not unless Mr. Landover told her, because I sure didn't."

"When's the last time you saw the jewels?"

"The last I saw them was the day I brought them to the Landover estate for the wedding. I'd cleaned them, as Mr. Landover asked the day before. And he had a security guard on me the whole time. Anyway, once they were clean, I brought them straight to Kit."

"Okay. Keep me updated if anything changes."

Robinson took a drag. "Will do."

Kirkland left the shop and found Mackey leaning against his car, her arms folded over her chest. She was wearing a black suit today, with a crisp white shirt and her hair up. He realized he preferred her hair down. Still, even dressed in this uniform she looked sexy as hell.

"That was cold," she said, pushing away from the car.

He moved around his car to the driver's side. "What, blowing your lie?"

"If the situation were reversed, I'd have played along."

"I did play along last night."

Color rose in her cheeks. "We're talking about business."

He shrugged. "Okay. Drop this case, Mackey." He unlocked the door. A gust of wind caught her perfume, and again he was treated to the very feminine scent.

"If anything, your renewed interest has really sparked my curiosity. You're not one to waste time on a case that's unsolvable."

"This case might very well go unsolved unless someone involved in Kit's murder makes a mistake."

She lifted a brow. "We keep assuming that someone killed Kit. What if she wanted to disappear?"

"You're forgetting the blood found in Landover's backyard. Over five pints, by the coroner's estimate. And DNA matched it to Kit Landover."

She twisted her necklace as she stared at him. He could almost hear the gears turning in her head. She'd found something out and was debating whether or not to tell him.

She pulled a rumpled piece of paper from her briefcase. "I received this yesterday."

"What is this?"

"It's the file of a grifter and prostitute named Brenda Latimer. Someone had it hand-delivered to my desk at the paper yesterday."

"Did you say Brenda?"

"Look at her picture."

He unfolded the paper and looked at the picture. Mild indifference turned into keen interest.

"She looks like Kit, doesn't she?"

"Some."

"Some! Dye the hair blond and add a couple of years and you've got Kit. I'm willing to bet money that Brenda reinvented herself into Kit."

His eyes narrowed. "A bit far-fetched. You know Landover must have had her investigated."

"Maybe he did look into her past. Maybe she was so beautiful he was willing to forget about it all."

"Maybe."

"Okay, just for the sake of argument, let's assume Kit was Brenda and she did assume a new identity. What if she didn't die that night but decided to reinvent herself again?"

Interest sparked in his eyes. "Possibly."

"Kit would use the same identity-building technique that Brenda used the first time. The more I can find out about Brenda the more I'll be able to figure out where Kit is now."

"*If* she's still alive." He shoved out a breath. "I'm listening."

She turned. "A new identity requires a birth certificate, preferably of someone who is a similar age and who died out of the country. Scanning the obits can tell you this. Once you've found your person, it's a simple matter to request a birth certificate from the state. If the kid didn't have a social security number, then you apply for one. If they did have a number, you take it."

"Are you going to New York to look into Brenda's past?"

"No, I'm headed to the town where she grew up. Cadence, Massachusetts."

"It is a small town on the ocean. I've been there before." He nodded. "Cadence is an area she's familiar with and it would be easy for her to steal more identities of the dead."

Mackey seemed glad that he was on the same page she was. "Exactly. Which is why I'm leaving first thing in the morning."

He didn't like the idea of her going alone. "Before you leave town, I have an idea."

"What?"

"There's the Founders' Ball tonight at the club."

She visibly cringed. "I remember. It's Regina's big thing."

Alex noted the tension in her voice. "I've been invited and Pierce Landover is expected to be there."

Her eyes narrowed and she moved toward him. "Is your short-term memory on the fritz? I was thrown out of that club yesterday."

"I'm not suggesting you sneak in the back door. I was suggesting you walk in the front door."

She folded her arms over her chest. "And how am I supposed to do that?"

"Be my date."

"Excuse me?"

He looked almost embarrassed. "My grandmother has been after me to attend this function for years. I've been doing my best to ignore her. But if you come, then maybe our presence will ruffle a few feathers. Maybe Pierce will open up."

"Oh, we'll ruffle a few feathers. *My type* sticks out at those places like a gorilla in a china shop. And I can't guarantee my temper."

He lifted an eyebrow. "Not even for a chance to talk to Pierce directly?"

She chewed her bottom lip. "It's tempting, Detective."

Alex swallowed a smile. "So you're in?"

She bit her bottom lip. "I don't do well around rich people."

"Afraid?"

The challenge in his voice had her hackles rising. "No."

"Good. Then find something nice to wear and be ready by six this evening. I'll pick you up at Roxie's."

She hesitated, clearly chewing on the idea. "Okay."

Chapter 8

Tuesday, July 15, 5:55 p.m.

Tara was in a blind panic. She'd changed her clothes four times in the last hour. Frustrated by her own vanity, she refused to look in the mirror again or second-guess what she was wearing now. She grabbed her slim black purse and headed down the stairs.

Roxie was at the bar polishing glasses. "Sounded like a hurricane upstairs. What's going on?"

The place was filling up with customers, and Roxie was at the bar mixing a Tom Collins and a pink lady. She handed the drink order to her waitress

Martha, a University of Boston student who worked full-time and carried a full premed schedule. Martha had brown hair that brushed her jawline and pale skin. She wasn't a great beauty, but to call her just average would have been unjust.

Martha tossed a grin at Tara as she loaded up her drinks. "Hey, girl." She took a long second look at Tara. "Wow, you look nice."

Tara glanced down at the simple black sheath dress. It was a top-of-the-line designer piece that she'd bought on sale a couple of years ago in Washington. She wore a vintage circle pendant made of small rhinestones, matching drop earrings and sling-back pumps. This was one of her few formal outfits, she dragged it out for business functions. "Thanks."

Martha raised her tray. "Be right back. No gossiping without me."

Roxie leaned forward. "So what's got you all twisted in knots?"

"I was trying to find the right outfit to wear. Detective Kirkland, I mean Alex, is picking me up and we're going to the yacht club for a party."

Roxie lifted a brow. "Very fancy."

"Yeah, tell me about it. My stomach is in knots."

"So skip the party and just go out to dinner."

"The whole point is to go to the party. He's kind of helping me with the Westgate story. I'm more likely to get a quote from one of Kit's friends if he gives me an introduction."

Roxie seemed pleased that Tara was even going out. "Well, don't spend the whole evening thinking about work. Not when you've got the attention of Detective Good-Looking."

Tara groaned at Roxie's description of Kirkland. "This is business."

Martha reappeared and set her tray on the bar. "What's business?"

"I'm working on another article. The Kit Landover disappearance."

Roxie shook her head. She caught the eye of a patron at the end of the bar who wanted a refill. "Martha, tell Tara she works too hard. Tell her to have fun."

Martha laughed as Roxie walked away. "I'm the original workaholic. I'm hardly one to give advice. So tell me about the story."

Tara was grateful to forget about country clubs and clothes as she filled Martha in on the details of the article. "Tomorrow I head to Cadence to see what I can find in Brenda's past."

"Should be a nice day for it."

"With luck, I'll only be there a day or two."

Martha noticed two new patrons enter. "Back to the salt mines."

Tara grabbed another handful of nuts, then thought better of it. She dumped them back in the bowl and decided to head outside and wait for Kirkland. With a wave to Roxie and Martha, she escaped outside. The sun was still bright but the heat of the day had eased off. The streets were full of patrons heading into shops, restaurants and bars. Summers were short in Boston, and people tended to make the best of them.

"Perfect timing." Alex's rich voice sounded behind her.

She turned to see him walking down the block. His gait was a bit uneven, but otherwise he looked fit and healthy. He was dressed in a dark suit and, judging by the cut and the fabric, she guessed it was handmade. A crisp white shirt set off a red silk tie. Evening light cast a warm glow on his face, accentuating the faint lines around his eyes and the firm set of his jaw. He looked—dashing.

Tara's unease grew. "I'm underdressed."

He shook his head. "You look fine."

She'd sworn she wouldn't fish for compliments, but nerves had her asking, "You're sure?"

"Absolutely. Don't worry about it." He smiled. "My car's parked up the street. It's the closest spot I could find."

She walked beside him up the street. "It gets a little hectic around here in the evenings. The tavern is always full."

He glanced back at the pink neon sign that blinked

Roxie's. Music spilled out from the bar's open door and mingled with the laughter of patrons. "She's got herself a gold mine," he said.

"And she knows it. The woman can manage a business."

Alex pulled out his keys and clicked the keyless remote. The lights on a sleek black BMW coupé flashed. He opened the door for her.

She sank onto the plush leather seat. The car was top-of-the-line, fully loaded, and she couldn't begin to guess what it had cost him.

He slid behind the steering wheel and fired up the engine. The muscle car engine purred.

Tara felt out of her element and found herself falling back to something familiar. She chose to talk about work. "Has the doctor who shot you gone to trial yet?"

He frowned. Clearly this wouldn't have been his first choice of topics. "Two weeks from now. It's going to be long, drawn out and will eat up a lot of my time."

"Don't be surprised if you see me in the courtroom. My editor likes the way I cover trials." She smoothed her hand over her dress, wishing she had something more formal.

"Honestly, it'll be nice to see you there. I could use a friendly face."

"I hear cops have a hard time of it after shooting someone."

His long fingers wrapped over the gearshift. He

downshifted as he switched to the turnpike exit. "You have a gift for asking uncomfortable questions."

"Sorry. It's in my nature. Tell me to shut up anytime you like."

He was quiet for a moment. "I don't mind the questions. I'm just not used to them."

"Leave it to a Mackey woman to bring up a delicate subject."

He sped up and moved to the left-hand lane. The car hugged the road like a race car. "You definitely keep me on my toes."

"I'll take that as a compliment."

He tightened his hand on the wheel. "Now it's my turn to ask the questions."

"I'm good at asking, but terrible at answering."

"It's only fair."

"Go ahead."

He grinned. "Why did you move up here from D.C.?"

"That's no mystery. Roxie. She turned sixty-five this year. And though she'll tell you she hasn't missed a step, I know running the bar is a bit of a grind for her. When I'm in town, I can open or close for her a few nights a week so she can get to bed early."

"What took you to D.C. in the first place?"

Tension washed over her. There was a topic that she didn't want to explore. "A job opportunity."

He shot her a glance. "And?"

"That's all I'm willing to comment on." She smoothed her hands over her skirt. Time to change the topic. "Isn't there something more important we could talk about, like whom I'm going to be meeting tonight?"

"I'd rather find out why you went to D.C."

"No comment."

He got off the turnpike in an exclusive area near the bay. "Okay, if you want to talk shop we can."

"Great."

"Just about everyone there tonight has crossed paths with Kit. Good chance someone might say something to you."

"Do you really think they'll talk to me?"

"I'm betting you'll hear more than me. People really clam up around cops."

"With this set of people, I think they're just as tight-lipped around reporters."

"We'll see."

Ten minutes later Kirkland pulled into the tree-lined circular driveway of the club. He put the car in Park but left the engine running. As Tara reached for the handle of her door, an attendant in a red jacket appeared and opened it for her. She felt a little silly as she got out of the car. "Thanks."

The bushes twinkled with small white lights, and soft music and laughter drifted from inside. It wasn't the bawdy, raucous sounds of Roxie's but instead had a cultured air that had her spine straightening.

Kirkland came around the front of the car and pressed his hand into the small of her back. He frowned. "Why are you so tense?"

"I told you, I don't do rich people."

"I'm rich." He said the words as if he were talking about the color of his tie.

"It's a major strike in your corner," she said honestly. "If you weren't such a good cop I'd have turned you down for this evening out."

That shocked him. "You mean you wouldn't date me because I have money?"

"It's not the money so much as how the money changes people. It can make them very selfish. The world of the rich is a place I want no part of."

Shaking his head, he guided her inside. "You're an odd duck, Mackey."

Tara smiled. "I've been called worse."

Kirkland guided her into the main room. A five-piece band played pop music. There was a full bar and a huge buffet of food, which no one seemed to be eating. Groups of well-dressed people filled the room, each wearing their designer gowns and diamonds.

Tara was suddenly aware that her outfit was an end-of-the-season-sale bargain three years ago, and that her pendant was rhinestone.

Kirkland seemed to sense her anxiety. "Would you like a drink?"

"Absolutely. Maybe two."

He grinned. "What would you like?"

A beer. "I don't know, what do people drink at these things?"

He shrugged. "Whatever they want."

"I'd love a beer."

"Preferences?"

"Whatever's on tap."

"Be right back."

She didn't want to be alone in this crowd. But she caught herself. She was here to meet people, to ask questions, and she *wasn't* going to be intimidated. "Great."

As he walked away and left her in the center of the room, she resisted the urge to follow him or stand behind a ficus tree in the corner. These people put their pants on just like regular people.

"Tara Mackey?" Regina Albright's cultured voice cut through the chatter.

Tara turned, smiling broadly. Regina was dressed in a pale blue silk gown. Her smooth blond hair was pulled back in a French twist and a stunning diamond-and-pearl choker hugged her pale, delicate neck. "Ms. Albright."

Regina pouted. "Please, call me Regina."

"Right. Regina." Tara tried to picture this woman

and Kirkland saying their I-dos. Before tonight, she couldn't have pictured it. But seeing him in his suit, she realized they must have made a beautiful couple.

"Love your outfit," Regina said.

"Oh, thanks."

Regina smiled sweetly. "That look was so hot a couple of seasons ago."

The gloves were off, Tara thought as she stared into the woman's frosty blue eyes. "So I hear."

Regina sipped champagne from a delicately fluted glass. "Maybe we can shop sometime?"

"Oh, sure," she said, knowing Regina's invitation was as hollow as her compliment. Where was Kirkland and that beer?

Regina lifted a brow. "So what brings you here?"

"Alex invited me."

A hint of ice crossed her gaze before it vanished. "You two are becoming quite the couple."

"Not really. We just have a mutual interest."

"Which is?"

"Finding out what happened to Kit Landover." Tara studied Regina's face for her reaction.

Mild interest was all she revealed. "Alex was asking me about her yesterday. Why the sudden interest? It's been a year."

Tara countered the question with a question. "I thought you were good friends with her."

"Well, not *that* close. Kit wasn't the kind of woman who cultivated friendships with women."

Interviewing Regina started to settle Tara's nerves. She felt as if she were back in her own element. "I heard she was a very sensual woman."

"In a cheap sort of way." Regina tapped her manicured finger against the crystal flute.

Was that the hint of jealousy? "Were you at the wedding?"

"Kit asked me to be one of her attendants but I had to say no. I was scheduled to be out of the country."

"Did you hear anything about the wedding after Kit went missing?"

"According to my friend Eleanor, the Landover estate was stunning. Pierce has wonderful taste. And the weather was perfect. Even Kit was more lovely than usual. And of course the Landover gems were the talk of the night."

"And Kit seemed happy?"

"Eleanor said almost giddy. But a bit nervous. Eleanor figured the nerves were just a bride thing."

There was something more lurking behind her words. "But…" Tara prompted.

"She heard Kit arguing with someone in her room right before the ceremony. It was a man."

"Who was she arguing with?"

"I don't know. Eleanor didn't recognize the voice. When Eleanor called me to tell me about it the next day, Kit was already missing. We spent an hour on the phone trying to figure out who the mystery man was."

The slight tension in Regina's body language had Tara asking, "Does Alex know this?"

She shrugged and sipped her champagne. "He never asked."

"How'd you feel about Kit?"

Regina seemed surprised by the question, but then shoved out a breath. "I despised the bitch, and she can stay dead as far as I'm concerned."

Alex collected the frosted beer bottles from the bartender and headed back to Tara. She'd been talking to Regina for over five minutes and his ex's face was showing signs of stress. During their marriage, he'd seen the look often enough and knew it meant trouble.

He was halfway across the room when he spotted Gertie. When she met his gaze, the look of shock on her face was priceless. He knew he couldn't get past her without a word.

"Don't tell me," Gertie said. "Hell has frozen over."

Alex smiled. "Probably."

"Your mother and father would have flown back from Paris if they'd known you were going to attend."

"I didn't really know myself until today."

Gertie studied him with an assessing gaze. "What on earth are you doing here?"

"I brought a friend."

She lifted a slim white eyebrow. "Why?"

"Can't I come to the club just for the fun of it?"

That comment made her laugh. "You've never done anything for the fun of it in your life."

She was right. He was always so hell-bent on proving himself to his family and the department that his life had been absorbed by work. He'd had no personal life. But since the shooting, he'd realized something was missing. He wanted *more*. What that more was he couldn't have said until he kissed Mackey last night. "My friend is Tara Mackey."

"The crime reporter?" She stared past him at Tara for a long moment.

He wasn't surprised Gertie recognized the name. She read the paper cover to cover every day. "Yes."

"She's a good writer. I am fond of her work. She doesn't treat you with kid gloves in her articles."

He smiled, noting he liked that about her. "No, she does not."

Gertie's eyes widened a fraction. "So why is she here? Please tell me she is a real date."

"She's not exactly a date," he said with some regret.

"She's here to ask questions about Kit Landover," Gertie said.

He'd never underestimated how sharp his grandmother was. "Yes."

"I'd heard there was a reporter at the club yesterday." Gertie glanced over at Tara. Approval shone in her eyes. "She seems to be handling her own with Regina."

"She's smart as a whip."

His grandmother nodded thoughtfully. "I'm glad to see Tara has done so well for herself. I always liked the girl."

Alex's interest peaked instantly. "I didn't realize you knew Tara."

"She dated Robert Stanford when she was in college. He brought her here often. He was over the moon for her and gave her an engagement ring. Then, when everyone thought they'd marry, he broke off the engagement. Seems his family didn't approve of her. After that, she moved to Washington, D.C., and I didn't see her again until you were in the hospital."

Alex didn't know which statement surprised him more. "Wait a minute. Tara was at the hospital when I was there?"

"She checked in on you several times. She never came into your room, but I overheard her speaking to the doctors."

Alex turned and looked at Tara, as if seeing her for the first time. She'd never told him she'd come to the hospital. For reasons he couldn't quite explain, that meant a lot to him.

He cleared his throat. "And you're telling me she

was engaged to Robert Stanford of the Mayflower Stanfords?"

"It's not general knowledge anymore but yes, they were engaged."

The benign dislike he'd harbored for Stanford over the years morphed into distaste. "And he dumped her?"

Gertie smiled at his accurate evaluation of the situation. "His mother didn't think Tara was suitable. And Robert always listens to his mother." She lowered her voice. "From what I understand, Mrs. Stanford tried to make a financial settlement on Tara. It was quite generous from what I remember. But Tara refused."

No wonder Tara had a chip on her shoulder. "How do you know all this?"

"Servants talk." Gertie's gaze settled across the room on Tara and Regina. "You better go intervene. I think Regina needs rescuing."

He glanced between the two women. They were as different as night and day. Regina was stunning and stylish and enjoyed her privileged life of cocktail parties, fundraisers and trips to Europe. And Tara said what was on her mind, didn't mind covering the toughest crime stories for the *Globe* and moonlighted in a bar at night to pay her college loans. In his mind, Regina paled next to Tara.

"I'll see you later." Alex kissed his grandmother

on the cheek and crossed the room. He stood beside Tara and handed her a beer.

She accepted it with a smile, but didn't drink. "Thanks. Regina and I were just having the most interesting discussion."

Alex doubted that. But he wanted to be closer to Tara. Except for his grandmother, she was the only other person in the room he cared about.

Regina looked visibly uncomfortable as Tara leaned toward her and asked, "So what did you and Kit talk about that last time?"

"Just girl talk. Nothing more." She glanced across the room as if someone had caught her attention. "If you will excuse me. It was lovely visiting, Tara."

Tara took a long drink of her beer. "Did you know that Regina hated Kit?"

"Doesn't surprise me. At one time Regina had her sights set on Pierce, and then Kit came to town."

"Was she a suspect in your investigation?"

"She had an alibi. Regina was in Europe when Kit vanished." Alex raised his beer to his lips and paused when he caught sight of Robert Stanford. "Heads up."

Tara turned to see Robert and his wife headed their way. Her face tightened only a fraction as she squared her shoulders.

His slim, athletic frame hadn't softened in the last

nine years and his blond hair was still thick. He rested his hand on the arm of the petite brunette, who was visibly pregnant. Tara could live with the fact that he hadn't gotten fat or gone bald, but knowing he was about to be a father stung some. They'd talked about having children once.

Robert beamed as he approached. "Tara, is that you?"

She refused to show hints of the angry young woman who nine years ago had called him a coward as she'd stormed out of his parents' home. "Robert."

Kirkland moved a fraction closer to her. The gesture felt protective, and she realized he knew about her relationship with Robert. Boston society was a small world.

Still, she was grateful for Kirkland as Robert leaned forward and kissed her on the cheek. He still wore the same aftershave.

"You look great," Robert said as his gaze skimmed her frame.

She smiled. "So do you."

"I read your articles. They're good."

"Thanks."

Robert's gaze shifted to Kirkland. "Alex, I never see you at these things."

Alex's expression was flat, as it was when he was interviewing a suspect. "Tara and I thought it would be fun."

Robert lifted a brow. "You and Tara are dating?"

The brunette cleared her throat. "Robert. Are you going to introduce us?"

Robert glanced at his wife and had the good sense to look embarrassed. "I'm sorry, this is my wife, Debra. Debra, this is Tara."

"Tara?" The extra emphasis on her name told Tara that Debra knew of her husband's history. "How nice to finally meet you."

Tara had never been good at small talk. "So when is your baby due?"

Debra's hand slid proudly to her belly. "November. It's a boy. He's our fourth child."

"Fourth? That's nice."

"The girls are eight, six and three."

Emotion tightened Tara's throat. Robert must have married Debra within months of their breakup. "Lovely."

An awkward silence settled between the four, and finally Robert cleared his throat.

"Tara," Alex said. "Ready to see my sailboat? I did promise you a tour."

She grinned brightly at him. "I thought you'd forgotten."

Alex glanced at Stanford. "If you'll excuse us."

Stanford nodded. "Sure."

Alex didn't bother with goodbyes, and seemed glad to see them go. He escorted her through the crowded room out onto the club's patio. Stars twinkled in the sky above and danced on the calm waters of the bay. The air was warm but had lost the biting heat of midday.

Outside, Tara felt as if she could breathe. She stared out on the water at the sailboats moored on the docks. Their sails were down for the evening and their tall masts jutted proudly toward the sky. Most of the boats looked as if they could sleep eight to ten people.

Tara took a long sip of her beer. "So who told you about Robert?"

"My grandmother," Alex said without apology. He stood close to her, staring out over the water.

"Good news travels fast."

"If it's any consolation, Stanford is an idiot."

That did make her smile. "Thanks. And thanks again for being a stand-in date."

"No problem, Mackey." He sipped his beer.

"So do you really have a boat?"

"I do."

"Which one is yours?"

"The one at the far end." She followed his outstretched arm out to a seventy-four-foot boat moored in the last slip. Teak decks and brass accents gleamed.

"So does it sleep like twenty or thirty people?" she asked jokingly.

"Just six. Three staterooms and three heads."

"Wow." She took a long sip of her beer.

He stared down at her as if trying to read her thoughts. "You ever been sailing?"

"Not since Robert took me. I got seasick each time."

"That's because Robert didn't and still doesn't know what he's doing. You sail with me and you'll love it."

She glanced up at him. His gaze held no hint of humor. "That's what I'm afraid of."

"Sorry?"

"That I would like it too much."

A hint of a smile touched his lips. She realized several people were staring at them.

And then Alex's gaze rose and fixed on a point behind her. "And speak of the devil."

Tara turned and followed his line of sight. Pierce Landover cut through the crowd, his sights set on Tara. Alex had the urge to protect her, but checked himself. She might have appreciated the chivalrous gesture when Stanford had approached, but Landover was different. He was the man she'd come to interview and if Alex knew anything about Tara, she was a tough interviewer. Still, he decided to remain close.

Pierce stopped beside Tara and sipped his neat single-malt scotch. "I understand you are asking questions about my late wife."

Tara didn't flinch. "Yes, I am. I'm doing a story

on Kit for the *Boston Globe*. I had a few questions for you about Kit."

"I make it a policy not to discuss my late wife with the media."

Tara's head cocked a fraction. "You refer to Kit as your late wife. Her death was never proven. Do you believe she's dead?"

His lips flattened. "Yes, I do. And I'm in the process of having her declared dead. It's time I move on with my life."

This was news to Alex. The last he'd heard, Pierce had vowed never to stop looking until he knew what had happened to Kit.

"Any theories on what could have happened to her?" Tara asked.

"Whatever I know, I shared with the police. Now do us all a favor and drop this story."

Tara met his gaze. "I'm afraid I can't do that. In fact, the more people who warn me away, the more I have a tendency to dig in my heels." She barely took a breath before asking, "Do you have any idea what happened to the gems Kit was wearing?"

"No." Pierce studied Tara with an assessing gaze that reminded Alex of a cat toying with a mouse before the kill. "Ms. Mackey, Tara if I may."

"Sure."

"Tara. My wife was quite unstable. Beautiful, but very unstable. I was willing to overlook all her faults because I loved her. Her death was a tragedy. The furor around our wedding day has finally started to fade away and I don't want it stirred up again. Now, I've asked nicely. Next time I won't be so kind."

Alex's hackles rose. "That a threat, Mr. Landover?"

"A promise," Pierce said, his gaze shifting to Alex. "Stay out of my business."

Tara's gaze flicked to Alex as if she were annoyed by his sudden protectiveness. But as Pierce turned to leave, she blurted out, "Have you ever heard of Brenda Latimer?"

Pierce hesitated and frowned. "Who?"

"Brenda Latimer," she said carefully. She spelled the last name.

Alex watched Pierce's expression closely. As a cop, he'd learned not only to listen to what people said, but also concentrate on how they said it.

"No," Pierce said. He seemed genuinely bemused, but then he had a reputation as an accomplished liar. "Who is she?"

"A grifter and prostitute from New York," Tara said.

He arched a gray eyebrow. "Why would I know someone like that?"

Tara shrugged. "I've seen pictures of her. She looks a lot like Kit."

Pierce sipped his scotch. "We all have our doubles, Ms. Mackey."

"These two women could be twins," Tara interjected as he started to turn."

Pierce shook his head. "Don't start any nasty rumors."

"I only deal in hard facts."

His expression tightened. "You will only get one warning from me." He strode away.

Tara watched him leave as she sipped her beer. "That went well."

Alex didn't hide his surprise. "You've been a reporter too long not to recognize a serious threat."

"His threats are a good thing."

"How so?"

She tapped her finger against the side of her beer bottle. "I'm getting closer to the truth."

Trying to kill Tara last night had been an impulsive act.

Borelli had been so careful this past year to cover his tracks. But when the nosy reporter had come sniffing around, pure adrenaline and anger had driven him into action. He'd gone to the paper, and when he'd seen her leaving he'd followed her. His rage had overtaken him and he'd rammed her car.

It had been thrilling and exciting to see the fear in her eyes as her car had rolled off the road. It had also been maddening to see her climb out of the wreckage whole and healthy. It had been tempting to double back and take a second swipe at her but by then motorists had begun to stop and help her.

In retrospect, it was better she'd lived.

The last thing he needed was Detective Alex Kirkland breathing down his neck. The cop was smart and he'd figure this whole mess out if Borelli wasn't careful.

Borelli just needed to control his temper and stay calm. What was it Kit used to tell him? Keep your anger in check and your mouth shut.

Just a few more weeks and the waiting would be over.

Chapter 9

Tuesday, July 15, 10:00 p.m.

Tara relaxed back in her seat as Kirkland drove them back to Roxie's after they left the club. They talked on the ride back about everything and nothing and Tara found herself forgetting about Robert, Pierce and the fact that Kirkland was from their social set.

Right now, he was just a man. A very attractive man, who made her feel things she hadn't felt in a very long time.

He parked in front of Roxie's and shut off the

engine. They sat in the moonlight. He'd taken off his jacket and loosened his tie. Chest hair curled out from the vee of his shirt collar.

She wasn't in a rush for the evening to end. "Thanks again for taking me."

"You're not a bad date, Mackey."

"You're not so bad yourself."

She remembered the kiss they'd shared the other night. She wanted to kiss him again, and that insight scared her. She had vowed nine years ago never to enter the high-society world and she feared Kirkland would put her back there.

Tara grabbed the door handle with hands that trembled just a little. "I better get going."

He frowned. "What's the rush?"

"I've got a very early morning tomorrow." Not waiting for him to open her door, she got out. As she walked to the bar's front door, she pulled out her keys.

His car door opened and closed. His steady footsteps sounded behind her. "So what's your early morning call?"

She faced him. "I'm going to Cadence."

He wasn't surprised. "I figured as much. I'm coming with you."

The idea of traveling with him, alone, made her very uncomfortable because it was a recipe for sexual chemistry and disaster.

"Don't come, Kirkland. It's not worth your time.

I'll only be gone a day, and when I get back I'll report back to you."

He leaned a fraction closer, forcing her to press her back against the door. He appeared in no rush to end their evening, nor did he seem to be in the mood to argue. "I like to do my own legwork."

"I don't have a partner."

Kirkland was so close Tara could feel his warm breath on her cheek. A hint of his aftershave mingled with his scent. "You looked great tonight."

That caught her off guard and her defenses rose. "Did Regina ask you to find out where I got my vintage fake jewelry?"

His gaze darkened. "Regina is the last person on my mind right now." He touched her pendant. "I just liked the look."

Tara had a habit of not thanking people when she was given a compliment. "Thanks."

"You've got great legs."

The huskiness of his voice made her belly tighten with desire. She struggled to regain equilibrium. "So what is the deal with Regina?"

He shoved out a sigh. "Why?"

"I don't know. She's your ex. But I think she's still got a thing for you."

"I told Regina we are finished." He brushed an imaginary fleck of lint from her shoulder. His hand brushed her cheek. "And for the record, I don't have a thing for her anymore. We're done."

Her body tingled with the contact. It had been far too long since she'd had a man touch her. She didn't realize until this moment how much she missed being touched.

Kirkland tucked a stray strand behind her ear and then gently slid his hand to the back of her neck. Ever so gently, he edged toward her, testing to see if she wanted him to kiss her.

She did.

Tara leaned into him, anxious to know what he tasted like. Gently, she kissed his lips. They were soft, sensuous.

He deepened the kiss, pressing his lips harder against her and then coaxing her lips open with his tongue. She leaned her body into him, savoring the sensations exploding in her. This man knew how to kiss. He knew how to make a woman want.

She wrapped her arm around his neck and pushed her breasts against his chest. He pushed her gently back against the door. His erection pressed against her as he started to kiss her neck.

A low moan rumbled in his throat. It had a primitive quality that made her wonder what other sounds he could make if they went up to her room and made love right now. She splayed her fingers over his hard chest. The brushed cotton of his shirt covered a hard, muscled torso.

Kirkland's hand slid down her shoulder and brushed her breast. She hissed in a breath.

His even, white teeth flashed. "Do you like that?"

"Yes." She barely recognized the sound of her voice. "Yes."

This time when he kissed her he cupped her breast, and her nipples grew hard under the lacy silk bra she wore.

"I want you," he murmured against her ear. "I want to peel that dress off you and see what your skin looks like in candlelight." His voice had a roughness to it that she found even more titillating.

She'd never been moister and she'd never wanted a man inside her so much. What would one night hurt? How could an hour or two of mindless sex change her life so much?

Tara knew the answer. For some it might not matter but for her, sex had to be attached to emotional commitment. And she could become very attached to Kirkland if she didn't take care.

Tara pulled back, moistening her lips with her tongue. "I can't."

"What?" His voice sounded far off, lost in a mist.

"I can't do this."

He pulled back and looked into her eyes. There was no anger, just confusion. "Why not?"

"I can think of a million reasons."

Kirkland's brow knotted. "Name one."

"Because tonight would just be about the sex. And I don't do casual very well."

He traced her jawline with his callused thumb. "It would be good between us, Mackey."

Her gaze dropped to his lips and she was already sorry they'd not be sharing a bed tonight. "I've no doubt. In fact, I'd bet it would be great. But like I said, I don't do casual."

A sigh shuddered through him and he leaned his forehead against hers. "Okay."

Tara stared into his vivid eyes. "Thanks for not making a big deal out of this."

Kirkland pulled back and kissed her leisurely on the lips. She savored the taste, and despite her virtuous words she wasn't so sure she could live up to them.

When the kiss ended he pulled back. "You're going to dream about me tonight."

He was so full of arrogance it made her laugh. "I probably will."

"Good. I know I'll be thinking about you." He smiled and drew back. "What time do we leave in the morning?"

Her thoughts hadn't kept pace with his. "Sorry?"

"For Cadence. What time do we leave for Cadence?"

"Not we, *me*."

"I come or I'll bring you into the station for withholding evidence." His stance was still relaxed but she didn't doubt that he meant exactly what he'd said.

She stood a little straighter. "That's blackmail."

There was no hint of contrition in his gaze. "Yes, it is."

Her mind cleared. "I was planning on leaving early, so I could be in Cadence when the courthouse opened."

"Perfect. I'll pick you up at seven in the morning." He kissed her lightly on the lips one last time. He strode toward his car with the arrogance of a man very sure about himself.

Tara was ditching Kirkland.

She'd decided last night that she wanted to go to Cadence without Kirkland. This was *her* story. And she wanted to be the first one to crack it.

She knew he would be mad when he realized she'd left him behind. But if the information she found was valuable enough she might be able to talk her way out of jail.

She'd risen before dawn, dressed and eaten a quick breakfast. Clearing her throat, she picked up her briefcase and stowed it in the trunk of her rental car. Above, the stars had already started to fade and the first hint of the sun peeked over the horizon.

She expected this excursion to be just a day trip but experience had taught her always to expect the unexpected. So to be on the safe side, she had packed a few necessities in case it turned into an overnighter.

Just the thought that this trip could extend to morning shored up her decision to leave Kirkland behind.

The last thing she needed was to be stuck in the middle of nowhere, overnight, with Alex Kirkland.

Chapter 10

Wednesday, July 16, 6:48 a.m.

Alex pulled up in front of Roxie's minutes before seven and scanned the side streets for Tara's rental car. There was no sign of the red Jeep.

He knew in an instant that she'd left him.

That annoyed him and even pissed him off, but it didn't exactly surprise him. "Damn."

He shoved a hand through his hair. She was determined to go this case alone, regardless of the risks. The woman had guts, which he could have admired if she had the least bit of common sense.

His cell phone vibrated. He removed it from the cradle on his hip and snapped it open. "Kirkland."

"This is Brady."

Brady's shift didn't start until eight and for him to be calling this early meant some kind of trouble. "What's up?"

Brady wasn't put off by Alex's gruff tone. "Have you left the city yet?"

He stared at the empty spot where Tara's car had been last night. His irritation grew. "No."

"Good. You may want to stick around."

"Why?" His first inclination was to track Tara down.

"We've got a homicide in the north end."

Alex looked up through the car window at the quiet side street. "Something unusual about it?"

"Yeah. Remember Lenny Robinson, aka Frederick Robinson, the jeweler?"

He laid his head back against the headrest. "He was the guy that cleaned and marked Landover's necklace for his wife."

Brady nodded. "One and the same. He was shot point-blank last night in his apartment. Likely dead before he hit the floor. His store was cleaned out. Not a gem left in the place."

Kirkland swore. There could be any number of reasons why Lenny had been killed—he'd made enough enemies in the past. But Kirkland knew in his gut this had to do with Tara's article. "You have a forensics team there?"

"They should be here in the next hour. I'm holding the scene until they arrive."

"I'll be there in twenty minutes," Alex said.

He fired up the engine of his car and then dialed Mackey's cell. The phone rang six times and then went to voice mail. She always had her phone with her, and caller ID would have told her it was him. She was dodging him.

When the machine beeped he said, "Very slick, Mackey. But like they say, you can run but you can't hide. I will see you when you get back into town."

He rang off, remembering the dream he'd had about her last night. She'd been on the deck of his sailboat and she'd been naked. Pale moonlight had washed over her creamy skin as he'd lowered his body down onto her. He'd cupped her full, ripe breasts and stroked his hand down her flat belly. The boat had rocked gently. She'd moaned his name into his ear as he'd driven inside her.

"She's going to drive me insane." Alex snapped the phone closed and dialed a second number.

A police operator answered, "Communications."

"This is Detective Kirkland. I need you to trace the location of a cell phone."

"Badge and verification numbers, please," the operator said.

He gave the operator his badge number to verify

his identify. When she gave him the go-ahead, he rattled off Tara's phone number. "Find her for me."

"Is she in the state?"

"She should be headed north to a coastal town called Cadence. If you find her there, keep tabs on her. I want to know where she is at all times."

The officer agreed and signed off.

He moved into traffic. "Mackey, what have you stirred up?"

The streets of Cadence swelled with the cars of summer tourists who had filled the Main Street parking slots. Tara had to circle the block several times before she found a space two blocks away. A gust of wind caught Tara's hair the instant she stepped out of her car.

Tara cursed the fact she hadn't worn her hair in a ponytail. Kirkland had said he liked it down so she'd left it down even knowing she wouldn't see him today.

She grabbed her briefcase, fed the meter and started down the cobblestone sidewalk. Cadence was a tiny coastal town that had no doubt gotten its start hundreds of years ago as a fishing village. The old buildings had been restored and the place had a more upscale feel now.

She moved down the busy street past antique shops, a café and a hardware store before she reached the stone steps that led to the courthouse's large front door. She pushed through the doors.

During the two-hour drive, she'd decided to start with Brenda's birth records and then check to see if there'd ever been a Kit Westgate born in Cadence. Tara pulled off her sunglasses as her eyes adjusted to the dimmer light.

"Can I help you?"

She turned in the direction of the voice and found an older woman sitting behind a reception desk. The woman wore her gray hair in tight curls and had glasses that magnified vivid blue eyes.

Tara smiled as she moved toward her. "Yes, I've come to search birth records. Ms…"

"Mrs. Shoemaker." The woman nodded as she swiveled her chair around toward a computer screen. "We don't get much call for that around here."

Tara didn't doubt it. She imagined there were few year-round residents left in this town. "I'd like to do a search on a Brenda Latimer."

Mrs. Shoemaker nodded. "I knew the Latimer family. They were fishermen."

Tara took the seat across from Mrs. Shoemaker's desk, excited that she'd found someone who knew the family. "Brenda would be about thirty-two now."

"Yep, and her half brother Scott Martin would be about thirty-five."

"Is he still in town?"

She started punching keys on the computer and

then sat back and waited for the machine to process her request. "No. He left at least fifteen years ago."

"What about Brenda's parents?"

"Dead. Died eighteen years ago." The computer beeped. "Here are Brenda's records." She read off the woman's statistics and then hit the print button. "We went automated about ten years ago. 'Course our computer is outdated and slow by today's standards, but I'm happy to sit and wait on a slow computer rather than dig in the basement for dusty records."

Tara tried to look interested. "What can you tell me about Brenda?"

"Mind my asking why you want to know so much about her? I mean the girl's been gone about fifteen years from Cadence."

"I'm a writer for the *Boston Globe*. I'm doing an article on young girls who lose their way in the big city. I stumbled across Brenda's case file when I was working on another piece, and became intrigued."

Mrs. Shoemaker nodded sadly. "She's your typical story. Her folks were good, but they were poor and didn't have their sights past the few beers they could afford on Saturday night. Scott was the same way. But Brenda, she always wanted more. She went to school with my boy Tommy. Did real well. Sharp as a tack. Graduated two years early and decided to head to New York to make her fortune."

As Tara scribbled notes, she thought about the

photo in Brenda's police file. "How old was she when she left town?"

Mrs. Shoemaker scratched her head. "Sixteen."

"And she never came back again?"

"Not that I know of." The printer under the desk spat out a piece of paper and Mrs. Shoemaker handed it to Tara.

"Can you search one more record for me?"

"Sure."

"Kit or maybe Katherine Westgate."

Mrs. Shoemaker frowned. "That's the name of that socialite that vanished last year. I can tell you she wasn't born here."

"Could you just check to see if there is a Westgate name on file?"

"The name does not ring a bell. And I know just about everyone in this town who lived here the last fifty years."

"Please?"

The woman nodded and slowly typed the name into the computer and hit Enter. "Now what do you want with this gal?"

"I don't know. I've just got a hunch about her."

Mrs. Shoemaker leaned back in her chair. "You reporters still go on hunches?"

Tara smiled. "Sometimes that's all I've got to go on."

"I bet you see all kinds of crazy folks in your line of work."

"You have no idea."

The computer dinged again. "Here we go." Squinting, Mrs. Shoemaker leaned forward and read the screen. "Well, this little gal won't do you any good. Elizabeth Katherine Westgate died when she was two days old."

"What year was she born?"

She rattled off the year as she hit the print button. "Two years older than Brenda."

If Brenda had found a way to hack into this system and steal little Katherine's identity, then she could easily do it a second time. "Okay, one last favor?"

Mrs. Shoemaker stared over the edge of her pink half glasses. "You're asking a lot."

Tara leaned forward. "I know. I know. Just one more?"

"Fine. But one's all. It's about my coffee break and it's half-price donuts at Ernie's on Wednesdays."

"Can you search girls born within five years of Brenda's birth year who also died young?"

"Sure." Again, she henpecked out the letters. The computer started to click as it searched its data banks.

Tara tried to make small talk. "So you were born here?"

"All my life. Sixty-two years and counting. Been at the courthouse forty of those." The computer dinged and Mrs. Shoemaker leaned forward, squinting as she read, and hit Print. "You got two matches.

One is a Robin Johnson, died of crib death at five days. She was four years older than Brenda. And the other is Bess Conway, died at age seven in a fire. She was two years younger than Brenda." Mrs. Shoemaker nodded. "Now, Bess I do remember. That fire was a real tragedy. Whole family got out but Bess. Fact, Brenda would have known about it."

Tara scribbled down the names of the little girls who had all died so young. She thought about the people who had mourned those little girls and what they'd think if they knew their daughter's identities could have been stolen.

"Mrs. Shoemaker, you have been great. Thank you so much for your help." She pulled a twenty out of her wallet. "Lunch today is on me."

The older lady rose gingerly as if her knees hurt and handed Tara the other two birth records. "Well, thank you very much." She pocketed the bill. "So when can we read this article?"

"I'm not sure yet. Haven't put all the pieces together. But it should be very soon."

"Be sure to send me a copy."

Tara agreed and wrote down Mrs. Shoemaker's mailing address. She also got directions to the local high school that Brenda attended.

She drove past the city limits to the countryside, following Mrs. Shoemaker's directions. She pulled up to the square brick building adorned with deco letters that read High School. She headed inside to the administrative office. Within five minutes, she'd explained what she needed and was sitting in the library with a stack of yearbooks. She chose the years corresponding with Brenda's freshman and sophomore years. During her freshman year, Brenda was in the yearbook nine times. Brenda's bright, fresh face appeared in the drama club, the chess club, cheerleaders and several other groups. Hints of the woman Brenda was to become were so clear as Tara looked at her face.

By Brenda's sophomore year, she didn't appear in any clubs. She was pictured with her class but her smile was less vibrant. This Brenda looked more like the girl in the New York Police Department mug shot. It didn't take much to guess what had happened to Brenda when she'd arrived in New York. Her fate had been shared by countless other girls.

Tara photocopied the pages on the librarian's copier. Whatever had gone wrong, Brenda had decided to reinvent herself and she'd stolen the identity of a little girl from her hometown to do it.

And Tara would bet money that if Kit were still alive, she'd returned to the same well for a new identity. Being a crime reporter, she'd learned that even criminals were creatures of habit.

Tara had two names to search. Bess Conway and Robin Johnson. From her laptop she logged into the paper's server and searched the girls' names plus their place of birth. There was nothing for Robin Johnson. However, Bess Conway's name did have a hit. Bess Conway had a boat registered at a dock on Sable Point, Maine. The town was three hours north on a small peninsula.

If she hurried, she could make the town by nightfall.

Tara exited the library. The midday sun made her squint as she headed across the school parking lot to her car. She fished her keys out of her purse and slid behind the wheel. She grabbed her cell and checked to see if she'd had any calls.

She had three new calls. All were from Detective Alex Kirkland.

Tara tensed and ignored this call as she had his first and second.

But as she climbed into her car, she remembered his raspy voice from last night. "I know I'll be thinking about you."

She wondered if he had.

Chapter 11

Wednesday, July 16, 7:00 p.m.

Tara had driven straight from Cadence up the coast to Sable Point. She'd expected the trip to take a few hours. It had taken seven. There'd been backups and delays all the way up the coast, including a drawbridge that had opened for a sail boat. As she'd sat for a half hour waiting for the boat to pass by, she couldn't help but think of Alex. The boat's white sails flapped angrily in the growing winds.

By the time she reached Sable Point, dark storm

clouds, thick with rain, loomed above. A large storm was brewing in the Atlantic.

Sable Point was little more than a run-down fishing village, and it didn't look like the kind of place Kit Westgate would have fled to. Fiji or St. Moritz seemed more to Kit's tastes. But then, if her theory held true, Kit was only a fabrication of Brenda's and a place like this would have felt somewhat familiar to her. Cadence had been much like this place, twenty years ago.

The town's battered wood and stone buildings didn't possess the quaint charm that Cadence now had. Sable Point lacked picturesque inns and tiny seaside restaurants and seemed to tenaciously fight all pressures to welcome outsiders or join the twenty-first century.

Tara felt as if she'd landed on another planet.

She stopped at the town's sole stoplight, which swayed back and forth in the wind. It blinked red. Gusts blew over the hood of her car, making the vehicle rock and sway.

Lights burned in the window of a small diner attached to a motel, so she pulled into the parking lot. Peeling white paint covered the one-story clapboard building. A neon Miller Beer sign blinked in the large picture window streaked with humidity. Inside, she could see booths but no people.

She shut off the engine, grabbed her purse and dashed inside. Bells jingled over her head as she hurried inside. She glanced around the dark-paneled dining room. A half-dozen booths covered in aging red vinyl patched with duct tape lined the room. Hundreds of black-and-white photos covered the wall. An old radio cracked and spit out the noonday news, and the smell of overcooked green beans permeated the diner. There was no one in sight.

Tara glanced back at the door. The sign read Open.

"Hello?" she shouted.

After a moment's pause, an old woman pushed through the swinging doors behind the counter. Tall with hunched shoulders, the woman wore her graying hair in a thin ponytail. Her dark blue cotton dress washed out already pale skin. Stern lips flattened into a frown when she saw Tara. "What do you want?"

So much for warm welcomes. "Coffee. Food."

The woman grunted and pulled a greasy menu from under the counter. "Then sit."

Tara chose a seat with the least amount of patches so she didn't snag her pants.

The old woman returned with a thick mug full of coffee, a spoon and a small silver pot of cream. She set it all on the table in front of Tara. "It's fresh. Just brewed it five minutes ago."

"Thanks."

The woman lingered. "What brings you here?"

Tara hesitated. "I've come to see Bess Conway."

Suspicion burned in the old woman's eyes. "Why?"

Tara sipped her coffee. "Just have a few questions for her."

The woman planted an arthritic hand on her hip. "What kind of questions?"

She had no intention of sharing her theories about Bess/Kit/Brenda. If she could find the woman alive, the headlines and story would be priceless. "It's personal. Family business."

The old woman grunted. "Bess doesn't have any family. She keeps to herself. We hardly ever see her in town."

A woman in hiding wouldn't go out of her way to make friends or come into town much. "Can you tell me where she lives?"

"She lives at the east end of the peninsula in the lighthouse cottage. Follow the main road through town and it'll take you straight there. Can't miss it."

"There's a lighthouse here?"

"No. It vanished in a storm over a hundred years ago. But the cottage still remains. That's why it's called the lighthouse cottage."

"Great."

"You might want to wait until morning. The storm is going to make it hard going, dangerous even. The road to the cottage is steep and rocky. My inn's got a few vacancies."

"I'd really like to push forward. I've come a long way and want to talk to her."

"She ain't going nowhere," the woman said. "Everyone's gonna be stuck in town until the storm passes."

Tara hated being this close to Bess and not being able to speak to her. Outside the wind howled. The rain started to fall harder. Like it or not she would have to wait. "Where can I register?"

"My brother runs registration. Around the corner of the building."

Tara wasn't thrilled about going back outside, so she ordered coffee and a sandwich. While she waited she checked her voice mail again. Roxie had called. So had Miriam. But nothing from Kirkland. She wasn't sure if she was relieved or disappointed.

After she returned her phone calls and finished her sandwich and a couple of coffees, Tara drove around the building to the neon sign that read Registration. She parked and pushed through the glass doors. A lone clerk sat behind the counter. The man's back was to her and he was watching a game show on a small television.

The place had a creepy feel and she flashed back to *Psycho*, the Hitchcock movie. She thought of the lone female guest checking into a hotel only to be stabbed in the shower by the man running the inn.

Tara shook off the image. "I'd like a room."

The guy turned. He was in his sixties, and had thinning gray hair and stooped shoulders. He peered over the top edge of his reading glasses at her. "What on earth would bring you out here at a time like this?"

"I've come to visit a distant relative. Bess Conway."

He frowned. "I didn't know she had family."

"Yeah. I hear she keeps to herself. Can I have a room?"

He shrugged. "Sure. I got several to choose from."

She filled out the registration card he gave her. "You don't get many tourists here, do you?"

"We get a few bird-watchers in the summer and the stray tourist but, no, we don't get much in the way of visitors. Rocky beaches and bad weather don't appeal to most." He glanced at the card she'd filled out. "Boston? You've come a ways."

"Yeah."

He grabbed a key from the Peg-Board. It had a number six on it. "When you leave the office, go right and then up the stairs. It's the third room on the left."

"Thanks."

She picked up her bag and followed his directions. Exterior steps led to the second floor where the room doors faced the outside breezeway. Each room had a large curtained window by the door. She opened the door to room six, flipped on the light and closed the door behind her. She turned the dead bolt and locked the chain for extra measure. She then checked the shower stall to make sure it was empty. Satisfied she was safe, she sat down on the bed.

The room was basic—one double bed, TV on a dresser and a coffeemaker. She set down her bag and turned on the TV. She flipped through several channels before she found one that wasn't covered in static.

A few minutes later, she stripped and got into the shower. The hot water felt good on her still-aching muscles. A bruise darkened her left shoulder and her ribs felt a little tender. She flashed to the moment her car had tumbled over. A chill slid down her back. She'd been damn lucky.

She washed her hair and when the hot water started to dwindle, she got out and toweled off. After putting on an oversize T-shirt, she made herself a cup of coffee in the courtesy machine on the dresser.

She got into bed and focused back on the TV. There was no cable and the reception was poor due to the storm. After she'd watched two reruns of *The Brady Bunch*, she switched off the TV. Better to get a good night's sleep so she could head up to Bess's place early.

Outside howling wind and rain pounded her door. Nothing about this place was welcoming. "This is the Bates motel."

Tara cut off the light and laid her head on the pillow. The walls creaked as the wind whooshed. Shadows danced on the walls. It wasn't like her to get the creeps but Sable Point managed to do it.

She closed her eyes. She wasn't sure how much time passed before she drifted off into a restless sleep.

A rattling sound woke her. She sat up in her bed and shoved long fingers through her hair, trying to shake the sleep from her mind. She glanced at her hotel-room door and saw the knob turn. She jumped out of bed and pressed her ear to the door.

"Who is it?" she shouted.

There was no answer and the rattling door handle stopped.

Her heart hammered as she stood by the door in her bare feet. Cold air blew into her room from under the door.

Finally after several minutes of silence, she got the courage to push the window curtain back and peer out onto the breezeway. The storm had passed and the moon was high in the sky, casting shadows on the wall of her room.

There was no one outside.

Closing the curtain, she glanced at the clock on the nightstand. 10:42 p.m.

An unsettled feeling washed over her.

She got back into bed. But Tara didn't sleep very well for the rest of the night.

She dreamed about Kirkland. Of kissing him, smoothing her hands down his muscled chest and staring into his eyes, alight with a dark passion.

When Tara woke she felt stiff, tired and relieved the night was over. She got up, showered again and dressed, taking extra care with her appearance. This time she pulled her hair back in a tight ponytail.

If she was going to meet Bess Conway, she wanted to look professional. She checked her briefcase, pulled out the handheld video camera and rechecked the battery. She also made sure the flash of her digital camera worked, as well.

She glanced at the coffeepot full of cold coffee and then at her wristwatch. The diner downstairs would be open by now and she could snag breakfast before heading up the coastal road.

Tara grabbed her equipment and headed out, planning to lock her briefcase in the trunk of her car. As she came down the steps, she noticed a second car parked behind hers. She was completely blocked in.

"What kind of idiot parked that car?" Tara locked her bag in the trunk of her car and headed into the hotel's office.

A woman now stood behind the counter. She was tall, heavyset and had bleached blond hair. The nameplate over her right breast read Florence. Gum snapped in her mouth as she glanced up from yesterday's paper. "Can I help you?"

Tara approached the desk. "Tara Mackey, room six. There is a car parked behind my car. I'm completely blocked in."

Florence peered out the window. "Right. He arrived about two in the morning."

"*He* got a name?"

"We don't give out our guests' names."

Frustration ate at Tara. "So *he* is staying here?"

"Sure is." Florence lifted her paper and found a handwritten note. "You said your name was Mackey?"

Tara fisted her hands over her car keys. "That's right."

"He said for you to wait for him. He'd join you for breakfast by seven."

Tara glanced at her watch. It was ten to seven. She could think of only one guy who would drive to Sable Point and make a point to block her car in the lot. "Can you tell me what room Detective Kirkland is in? I have a message for him." She smiled, doing her best to keep her temper in check. "He and I work together."

With a name supplied, Florence shrugged. "Room five, the one next to yours."

The jagged edge of her room key dug into her hand as she tightened her fist. "Great. Thanks."

Tara pushed through the lobby door and climbed the steps to the second floor two at a time. She pounded on the door of room five, Inside she heard the TV's static reception of the morning news.

"Just a minute." Kirkland's baritone voice was unmistakable.

She beat on the door a second time knowing it would piss him off.

"Just a damn minute, I said." Kirkland sounded annoyed.

Good. She was tired, generally irritated and ready for a fight. Kirkland was one of the few who didn't mind going toe-to-toe with her.

The door snapped open. Kirkland stood dressed in long khakis and a white button-down shirt that he'd yet to fasten. Dark chest hair curled on a well-muscled chest and trailed down a flat belly to his black belt.

The wind in Tara's argument deflated a fraction and she had to regroup. She was aware of snapping her mouth closed and raising her gaze to meet his blue eyes.

Tara straightened her shoulders. "Why are you parked behind my car?"

Kirkland removed his hand from behind his back and she realized he'd palmed his .38. He released the hammer on the gun and visibly relaxed. "Good morning to you, Mackey."

She held out her hand. "How about you give me the keys to your car so I can move it? I'd like to be on my way."

The hint of a smile tugged the edge of his lips. "We'll head out to find Bess after breakfast."

"How do you know about Bess?"

He stepped aside so she could come into the room. "I've been following your trail since yesterday."

She moved into the room, careful not to touch him. He smelled of fresh soap. Nice. "How?"

He closed the door behind her. "Your cell phone signal. I had your location triangulated."

"I had it turned off most of the time."

"Yes. I know. I left you a few messages." He slid the gun into his hip holster and started to tuck in his shirt. "But on enough to emit a traceable signal."

Clever. He got points for that. "So you've been to Cadence."

On his bed was an overnight bag and beside that a shaving kit which appeared to be packed with brutal efficiency. "Sure have. Spoke to a nice lady at the courthouse in Cadence. Mrs. Shoemaker. She remembered you and she said to thank you again for lunch."

"Great."

He looked almost cheerful. "Are we here to see Bess or Robin? I didn't have a chance to run down the names. I fought the storm most of the way up."

There was no point lying about her lead. "I'm here to see Bess Conway."

He nodded. "I knew if I didn't delay you this morning you'd be up bright and early, just like you were yesterday, and out storming after your story." He slipped on a blue sports jacket. "I've got to hand it to you, Mackey. You've got a cop's instincts when it comes to finding the truth."

The backhanded compliment pleased her. "I told you I'd keep you posted on my findings."

"Then why did you ditch me yesterday? And why did you ignore my calls?"

"I haven't proven anything yet. There's nothing to report until I go up to that lighthouse cottage."

"We'll talk about that over breakfast."

His aftershave still lingered with the mist of his morning shower. He smelled good. "Let me just do my job, Kirkland. I don't need your help."

His expression turned deadly serious. "You need back up."

"Please, I'm a reporter, not a cop. I can take care of myself."

"You are after someone who most likely doesn't want to be found." From the top of the TV he grabbed his wallet, keys and loose change and pocketed them all. "I don't know about you, but I'm starving. Want to grab breakfast?"

She folded her arms over her chest. "I lost my appetite."

"You're not going anywhere until I do, so you might as well share breakfast with me. Besides, whoever you're after isn't going anywhere. I've got state police watching the bridges and roads. No one is getting in or out of town without me knowing it."

"Nice to have connections."

"Yes, it is." He shut off the TV and moved to within

inches of her. His thick, short hair was still damp from his morning shower. He'd just shaved but she knew there'd be a shadow on his jaw by late afternoon.

Her heart beat faster. She'd had her share of dreams about him last night. To play it safe, she moved to the door and opened it. "Let's grab breakfast. And you can fill me in."

"Share and share alike. Is that it?"

"Yes."

He pressed his hand into the small of her back and guided her out to the breezeway. He closed the door and double-checked the lock to make sure the door was secure.

Kirkland escorted her into the diner and they found a booth. The place was filled with the smells of coffee and bacon. A waitress in a yellow uniform served coffee to a grizzled local fisherman who had worn hands and stooped shoulders before she made her way to their table.

"Busted my truck up good," the waitress said to the fisherman. "The front headlight is broken and the fender is bent. He says he didn't take it out last night but I know he's lying."

The fisherman shook his head. "Teenagers will drive you to drink."

"Tell me about it." The waitress glanced in their direction. "Let me take care of these folks, Ezra. Be right back."

The waitress, a coffeepot in hand, came to their table. “Morning, folks. You want coffee?”

“Please,” Tara said. “High test.”

Kirkland nodded. “Same.”

The waitress grinned as she served each a cup. “Couldn’t do without my morning cup.” She set menus down in front of them. They each ordered the Number Two—pancakes, eggs and bacon. “That was easy. Be right back for your order.”

Tara glanced out the window at the parking lot as she sipped her coffee. Three spots down from her car was a truck with a banged-up front end. “That must be the car our waitress’s boy wrecked.”

Kirkland sipped his coffee. “Looks like about five hundred dollars worth of damage.”

“I wrecked Roxie’s car when I was sixteen. I did eight hundred dollars worth of damage. I washed dishes after school for six months to pay that one off.”

“Were you drinking?”

“Good Lord, no. Roxie would have tanned my hide. I backed out of the school parking lot too fast. I was in a rush to get to a debating tournament.”

He lifted a brow. “Actually, I can picture you on a debate team. I bet you were good it.”

“I was the captain. Arguing has always been a strength for me.”

The waitress brought their breakfasts, and as

Kirkland sliced into his eggs he said, "Fill me in on what you've learned so far."

"I'd rather not until I have more information."

"If you don't share, Mackey, we'll head back to Boston now and you can consider yourself under arrest for obstruction of justice." He spoke calmly, but there was steel in his voice.

She stiffened. She didn't doubt for a moment he'd do it. "You would not."

His gaze reflected resolute determination. "I'd do it in a heartbeat. And don't ever forget that I don't make idle threats. I want this case solved in a very big way and I'll do what it takes to see that it's closed."

The last thing she needed was to cool her heels in a Boston jail cell while Kirkland cracked this case. She wanted in on the story and if that meant she had to play ball she would.

Tara buttered her pancake and poured a healthy dose of syrup on it. She gave him the rundown on Brenda's past life in Cadence. "I'd have gone to see her yesterday if not for the storm."

Kirkland nodded as he peppered his eggs. "I'm glad you didn't."

"Afraid I'll beat you to the punch?"

His expression grew serious. "If this woman is Kit or Brenda, she's worked very hard to stay hidden. She might not think twice about killing a reporter who gets too close." He frowned. "Any more thoughts on who sent you the initial information on Brenda?"

"None. I reread the information last night but there was nothing." She cut into the pancake with her fork and took a bite. It tasted great and she ate half the plate of food before she realized it. "What time did you arrive last night?"

He'd eaten his entire meal. "About two."

"Right."

"Why?"

"Someone rattled my door last night about quarter to eleven."

He frowned. "Did you see who it was?"

Her stomach tightened. "By the time I got up the nerve to look out the window, whoever it was had left."

Kirkland shook his head, his gaze deadly serious. "I don't like this, Mackey."

"Who was trying to get into my room?"

"That's a good question. Did anyone know you were headed to Sable Point?"

"I told my editor." She tried to shrug off her worries over the incident. "It was likely a fluke. Someone must have gotten their room number mixed up."

"Don't bet on it."

Chapter 12

Thursday, July 17, 8:00 a.m.

After breakfast, Tara got her gear out of her trunk and put it in the back of Kirkland's car. The rain had stopped but the air was thick with humidity and the skies above remained dark and ominous. They were in for more rain and, according to Florence, this storm was supposed to be worse than yesterday's. Kirkland drove up the rutted coastal road toward Bess Conway's cottage.

Kirkland's broad shoulders ate up the space in the front seat of the car and Tara was very aware of him. Despite all her griping at breakfast, she liked having him close.

Tara couldn't shake her sexual attraction to the man. He dominated her thoughts far too much. She turned her gaze out the window. She was courting trouble—*big-time.*

To keep her mind off Kirkland, she stared at the desolate, rocky terrain. Sea oats blew over barren sand dunes. "Kit gave up the lap of luxury for this place. Why would she do it?"

"I don't know. But this would be about the last place I'd have looked for her. And I can't picture Pierce coming here, either."

Tara shoved out a breath, wishing Kirkland would drive faster. "If Bess is Kit, are she and Pierce still legally married?"

He shook his head as the car snaked up the rocky coast. To their right, the rough waves washed onto rocky shores one hundred feet below. "She married him under false pretenses, so who knows? An annulment is very possible. But that's a job for the lawyers."

Wind gusted over the hood of their car as Kirkland drove up the coastal road. She glanced out her window and realized they were a hundred feet above the rocky shore below, where waves crashed over jagged rocks.

He rounded a blind corner and slammed on the

brakes. The car skidded to a halt. Tara lurched forward, her seat belt catching her before she hit the dash.

Kirkland swore.

She glanced up to see a pile of rocks in the center of the road. They'd fallen from the hillside to the west. If Kirkland had been going any faster, he'd have hit the rocks and they could have tumbled over the edge.

Kirkland shoved out a breath. "That'll wake you up."

Tara tried to laugh off her own fear. Suddenly, she was very glad to have him with her. "Tell me about it. Can we get around it?"

He nodded. "Barely." He put the car in Reverse and backed up a hundred feet. Then, very carefully, he started forward, inching the car wheels round the rocks littering the road.

Tara wanted to close her eyes, but she forced herself to look out her window. They had just inches to spare before the shoulder of the road dropped off. "God, I hate heights."

Kirkland didn't take his gaze off the road. "I didn't think you were afraid of anything."

"I'm afraid of a lot of things. The trick is to not let the fear show."

He maneuvered around the rocks and had the car back in the center of the road. She breathed a sigh of relief.

The crisis had passed and Kirkland relaxed. Still, he kept his eyes forward and on the road in case there were other problems ahead. "So what else are you afraid of?"

She laughed, feeling her equilibrium returning. "Maybe another day."

"We've got a few minutes now."

"No comment." He was the last person she'd reveal her fears to.

"Just one."

"No way. A successful crime reporter needs a tough exterior. You better than anyone should know cops don't respect weakness. And I refuse to have any of you guys condescending or coddling me when I show up at the next murder scene."

There was a hint of understanding in his eyes. "I'll show you mine if you show me yours."

She laughed. "I can't imagine you being afraid of anything."

"Before the shooting I was just a little too cocky. My near-death experience, as you called it, gave me plenty to fear." His voice was quiet, pensive.

Tara wasn't going to tell him not to worry or toss platitudes his way. "I'm afraid of heights and closed-in spaces. Fear can be a good thing. It keeps us on our toes and reminds us that we don't control everything."

Kirkland tightened his hands on the steering

wheel. "On my toes I don't mind. Being crippled by fear does worry me."

She studied his jaw as it tightened and released. "You seem no worse for wear after the shooting."

He swallowed. "I've yet to draw my weapon or be tested again."

She smoothed her hands over her thighs. "Do you ever think about him?"

"You mean the guy I killed?" He shook his head. "I don't lose any sleep over shooting Dr. O'Donnell. He'd savagely killed his wife and he was trying to kill one of my men." He shoved a hand in his pocket and rattled the loose change. "But I worry that if I'd been a second slower, what would have happened to Brady? He's a damn good cop and has five kids at home depending on him. I also worry that if I ever have to fire my gun again I'll freeze or I won't be fast enough to stop the bad guy."

"You can't do that." Her voice had softened.

"Do what?"

"Play the *what-if* game. Believe me, I am the master at it and I can tell you that you'll drive yourself insane and get nowhere in the process."

A smile tugged at the edge of his lips. "You sound like the department shrink."

"No doubt he is a wise man."

"She's a wise woman."

She smiled. "Naturally."

Kirkland came around a final bend.

Tara leaned forward. "Bess's cottage should be about two hundred yards down the road."

Kirkland nodded. "Right."

Their conversation silenced, he pulled into a short dirt driveway furrowed with ruts caused by Sable Point's frequent rainstorms.

He followed the drive up to a small, gray stone house that looked older than the town, which had been settled around the turn of the nineteenth century. Dark shutters had been closed over the four windows that faced south. The garden had long been overgrown with weeds.

Kirkland parked the car and they both got out. A fine mist hung in the air and the clouds above were ripe with rain. "We better move fast or we're going to find ourselves trapped in one hell of a storm."

"Local weather said the second storm wasn't expected until later today."

Kirkland shook his head and unsnapped the snap on his gun holster. He started out ahead of her. "Don't bet on it. This storm is moving fast."

"So you're a weather expert?"

"I'm damn good at gauging the weather." He spoke with confidence, not arrogance, and she accepted him at his word.

Tara moved forward and almost immediately tripped over a vine that snaked over what was left of a brick pathway to the house.

Kirkland moved in front of her as they approached the front door. Weather had stripped most of the paint off and left the wood underneath cracked and swollen.

When she tried to step around him he held up his arm, blocking her path. "Stand to the side of the door."

She did, feeling a little foolish. "Is this really necessary?"

"Always assume that what's behind the door wants to kill you." He also positioned himself beside the door before he knocked. "Bess Conway."

They both stood in the morning silence, listening for any sign of someone inside. With the sun behind the clouds and the wind whipping, Tara was cold. She huddled a fraction closer to Kirkland to absorb his heat.

He pounded on the door again. "Bess Conway."

When there was no sound or trace that anyone was in the house, Tara moved to one of the windows. She opened the shutter and rubbed the salt-streaked window clean with her hand. She peered through the clean circle into the main room.

Immediately, Tara saw a woman.

She was lying face-up on the floor in a pool of blood.

Chapter 13

Thursday, July 17, 10:00 a.m.

Gun drawn, Alex twisted the door handle. It was locked. He kicked open the cottage's front door. "Mackey, stay outside."

She stepped toward him. "I want to come in."

"Stay *outside*." He didn't want to risk Tara's life. Three months ago he'd learned firsthand how dangerous a simple visit could be when the doctor had drawn on and shot at Brady and him. "We don't know who else is still here. Now stay put so you don't get us both killed."

She frowned but nodded. "Fine. But if you need me, call and I will come."

Mackey didn't have a gun but he knew she'd run into a fire to save him if he needed her. He offered a smile and then turned his focus to the cottage.

Every piece of furniture, every closet, every full-length curtain could hide a killer. He couldn't take anything for granted. His gun pointed forward, he scanned the room with his gaze, going left first and then right.

The room was simply furnished with a couch, end tables, lamps and a braided rug. Alex swept his gaze right and noted two doors. Slowly, he moved closer to each. He opened the first. There was nothing behind it but boxes. His heart pounded as he moved to the second. He flipped open the door, his gun pointed and ready to fire. No one.

He canvassed the entire house, methodically going from room to room, looking for the killer. The thorough search revealed no one. The place was clear.

He holstered his weapon and went to the woman's body. He squatted by her and gingerly reached down to press his fingers to her neck. There was no pulse. Her skin was cool but her limbs were stiff and rigid, as they would be if rigor mortis had set in. It hadn't been long since she'd died.

The victim's long dark hair covered her pale face. He gently brushed back her hair and for a long moment just stared. It was Kit. There was no mistaking the high cheekbones, full lips and aquiline nose.

He rose and moved to the front door. He didn't want to contaminate the scene any more than he already had.

Tara waited by the front door. For the first time, she'd actually listened to him and stayed put. And then he saw the camera in her hand. She'd gone to the car to retrieve it. "There's no one in the house."

She stared through the open front door. "Is it Kit?"

"Yes."

Her eyes widened with interest and shock. "I was *right.*"

"Yeah. You nailed this one."

She raised her camera and started taking pictures. Alex placed his hand in front of her lens. "No pictures, Tara."

"But this is *huge,* Kirkland. We can now prove that Kit didn't die on her wedding day. She's been living here for a year. We were the first to figure it out."

"Apparently we weren't the first."

Her brows knotted. "How do we know the killer knew of her true identity?"

He shook his head as he pulled the cell from its cradle. He dialed the sheriff's number. "Someone killed Frederick Robinson, the jeweler, yesterday. A gunshot wound to the head. His place was robbed."

Mackey frowned as her mind turned over the possibilities. "This place hasn't been robbed."

"No."

"Do you think I was set up?"

"What do you mean?"

"Set up to find Kit. Someone knew about her past and they gave me just enough information to find her so they could kill her."

That thought didn't please him. "You could be right."

"I want to have a look around the house."

"No. Stay here while I call this in."

Tara had no intention of staying put. When Kirkland started talking to the state police on his cell phone and turned his back to her, she eased back around the corner of the house. She wanted to see where Kit had lived this past year.

She carefully picked her way through the weeds and briars as she moved around the house's stone corner. One hundred yards ahead was a cliff that dropped to the sea. The roar of the ocean below mingled with the rush of the wind. And in the distance, a dark, angry sky loomed over the whitecaps dotting the choppy sea.

What a sad, lonely place this was. This island hilltop stood in sharp contrast to the cheeriness of Cadence, the glitter of high society and even the busy streets of New York. What had brought Kit here to this place that felt more like a prison than a refuge?

Tara found a narrow path that led to the edge of the cliff and she followed it halfway and then turned back toward the house. She snapped more pictures of the house and of the view of the ocean. Miriam was going to be blown away when Tara gave her a full report.

Tara continued down the path. Several times she had to stop as the briars caught her pant leg and snagged the fabric. When she reached the edge, her heart hammered in her chest.

She sucked in a deep breath and peered over the edge. Sea spray blew in her face. Fifty feet below, waves washed over jagged rocks. Gulls squealed.

Tara started to draw back when she caught sight of something on the rocks. It was the flutter of white fabric. She squinted and stared hard at the rocks. And then she slowly realized what she was looking at.

It was a dead body.

A man, dressed in a white shirt and black pants. Suddenly she remembered Borelli two days ago. He had been wearing a white shirt and dark pants.

Strong hands grabbed her. It was all it took to shatter her frayed nerves, and she screamed.

"What the hell are you doing?" Kirkland whipped her around and stared at her as if she'd lost her mind.

She'd never been so glad to see anyone as she was

him. Without thinking, she hugged him. Automatically his arms came around her waist and he drew her to him.

His embrace felt warm. *Safe.*

She swallowed and got control of her racing thoughts. "There is another body on the rocks below."

Within an hour the local sheriff had secured the area and had called in the state police. Because of the victims' identities, the state coroner had been flown in by helicopter to handle the bodies. A police boat had also been sent and officers below were now securing the dead man's body.

Everyone was hurrying as fast as they could to gather as much evidence as possible because when the rains came, the evidence would be destroyed.

Tara had been relegated behind the yellow tape while Alex spoke to the local sheriff near the front entrance of Kit's house. Tara had to lean forward and concentrate to eavesdrop on their conversation.

"Have you seen anyone unusual coming and going on the island?" Alex asked.

The sheriff was in his late fifties, had a potbelly and liked to chew tobacco. His uniform was rumpled and his hat pushed back on his head. "Nope. Can't say that I have."

Tara was good at reading people. She could see that the sheriff was feeling intimidated by the arrival of a big-city cop and state officials. Alex too seemed to sense this, and was doing his best to put the officer at ease.

"The drawbridge road is the only way in and out of the island?" Alex asked.

"If you're driving a car."

"And if you're not?" Alex said patiently.

"Well, then I guess you could moor in a dozen different spots on the peninsula."

Tara couldn't resist a question. "What's the closest docking spot to this cottage?"

Alex frowned. He didn't like anyone running his investigation either. But he nodded. "It's a good question."

The sheriff directed his answer to Tara. "Miller's Cove is the closest. It's about a half mile from here. But I'll tell you, it's not for the weak. Whoever came up that way would have to scale a big drop-off."

"Any other spots?" Tara asked.

"Yep. I can think of two others off the bat."

"I'll need those names."

The rainy mist was growing heavier and seeping into Tara's shirt. The spray combined with the breeze from the ocean was chilling her to the bone. It was the middle of July and she was freezing. She could have escaped to the warmth of Alex's car, but that would mean she'd miss out. And she'd rather freeze than miss anything.

"Better get an officer down to those docking spots

soon," the sheriff said. "When this storm comes, it's gonna wash out whatever evidence there is."

Alex frowned and then directed two state police officers to get with the sheriff and check out the coves. When the sheriff and the officers had left, Alex glanced toward Tara. "Go sit in my car. You're going to freeze at the rate you're going."

She grinned. "No way."

The radio on the sheriff's hip squawked and he removed it from its clip. "Sheriff Profit, are you there?"

The sheriff pressed the walkie-talkie's side button. "Ten four."

"This is Sergeant Armstrong, state police. We have the male victim out of the water. Driver's license names the victim as a Marco Borelli. He has a gunshot wound to the head. He also has a bag of gems in his pocket from Robinson's Jewelers."

Tara wiped the mist from her eyes. Hell would freeze over before she left this place.

The rainstorm started with a few fat rain droplets but in minutes the droplets turned to a heavy shower. Alex glanced back at Tara. She was shivering and her skin was paler than normal. At the rate she was going, she'd catch her death if she didn't get out of the rain. As much as he wanted to let her into the house, he couldn't have any more contamination of the crime scene.

"Tara, get in my car," he shouted. "I'll join you in ten minutes."

Her red hair was plastered against her head and she was doing her best to protect her camera under her shirt. "I don't want to miss anything."

"You won't. The drama is over for the moment. And I promise to fill you in."

"Swear?" Her teeth chattered.

"I swear."

She nodded and hurried to the car.

Alex slipped on paper booties and rubber gloves and went into the house. There he was met by the state police chief, a tall, thin man with dark hair and a dour expression. His name was Patterson. He was new to the job, but had gained a reputation as thorough and exacting.

Though Alex had called in the body, the investigation fell into the local sheriff's and the Maine state police's jurisdictions.

Patterson watched as the coroner zipped up the body bag and sealed it. The seal wouldn't be broken until the body reached the state medical examiner's office. The attendants lifted the bag onto a gurney and led it out of the house. "I'll do an autopsy, but it looks like the gunshot wound to the head was the cause of death." He scanned the barren room. "I remember the stories about her in the *Globe* last year. Everyone thought she was dead."

Alex nodded. "That's what she wanted us to believe."

"How'd you find her?" Patterson asked.

"It wasn't me. I was going on a reporter's tip. I followed her here."

The coroner glanced out the window. "That the redhead who looked like she was turning blue?"

Alex nodded. "She's the one. Hopefully she had the sense to turn the heater on in my car."

Patterson rested his hands on his hips. "It's going to take my boys hours, if not days, to process this scene. We've got a few computers in a back bedroom that need analyzing, as well as prints and fibers."

"Did anything catch your eye that tells you who might have done this?" Alex asked.

Patterson smiled. "You mean like a smoking gun?"

Alex shrugged. "Would be nice."

"Not so far, but if we find anything I will let you know."

"We had a murder in Boston yesterday—Frederick Robinson, a jeweler with a sordid past. He was shot with a .45." Alex hit the highlights of Robinson's sordid past.

Patterson nodded. "Does Robinson have anything to do with the gems found on Borelli?"

"I think they were from his shop."

"Okay. When I have more, we'll compare notes."

"Thanks."

Patterson shoved out a breath. "My guess is that Kit was planning to vanish for a good while. All that blood on the estate would have taken months to collect."

Alex nodded. "She knew five pints splashed around the greenhouse would lead everyone to believe she was dead." He thought about the picture of her from the New York PD. "The woman was a master at reinventing herself."

"So why leave a billionaire for this godforsaken rock?"

"That's the mystery."

Tara was thrilled to see Kirkland emerge from the cottage. She'd been in the car ten minutes with the heat blasting, but she couldn't shake the cold from her bones. And she was anxious to ask him questions.

Kirkland ducked under the yellow tape and came up to the car. He shrugged off his jacket, tossed it in the backseat and got in behind the wheel.

"So what's going on?" she asked.

"There's nothing more for us here now. It's going to take the state police time to figure out what they have."

"We're just leaving?"

"It's a Maine state police crime scene. Out of my jurisdiction."

"You're just giving up."

"No. I'm turning it over to other professionals."

"The Alex Kirkland I know would never walk away from a murder scene."

He shook his head. "I'm not walking away from anything. I'll be back as soon as this rain lets up."

Teeth chattering, she nodded. Tara held her cold hands out toward the vent. The pit-pat of rain droplets on the roof grew stronger. "So what can you tell me?"

He turned sideways and draped his arm over the seat back. "Honestly, not much to tell yet. But I promise, as soon as I can release any information, you will be the first to know."

"Promise?"

"Yes. Now let's get back to the motel."

When he smiled, wrinkles formed at the edges of his eyes. Her heart skipped a beat and she remembered the kiss they'd shared the other night. Strong sexual desire surged through her. She wanted to kiss him again. She wanted to touch him.

Tara shoved out a breath. "Sounds good."

They drove down the jagged road and discovered the sheriff had cleared the pile of rocks they'd almost crashed into earlier this morning. Fifteen minutes later they were standing outside their motel-room doors.

"Take a hot shower," Alex said. His voice sounded husky, as if he were imagining her in that shower.

Despite the chill, warmth spread through her body as she stared at him. She was on the verge of offering to share that shower when she caught herself. Damn, what was wrong with her? Sex with Kirkland was a complication she did not need.

"Right," she said. She fumbled with her key and opened her door.

Closing the door behind her, she dropped her keys and purse on the now-made bed. She stripped off her clothes, draped them over a chair and turned on the shower. Steam filled the tiny bathroom as she stepped under the warm spray. She dipped her head under the showerhead, rinsing the cold rain from her hair. The warmth felt so good and she stood there for several minutes before the chill left her body.

Finally, she got out of the shower and wrapped her hair and body in towels. She clicked on the TV and settled on a channel with the least amount of static.

She switched on her laptop and started to write her article. This story wasn't even close to being played out but there was enough to sketch an outline. When she'd finished, she phoned her editor. Miriam picked up on the fourth ring.

"It's Tara, and boy do I have a story for you."

Tara ran down what she'd found out in the past thirty-six hours. Miriam listened, not saying a word or puffing on a cigarette.

"So how soon can you have copy?" Miriam said.

"I only have notes now."

"E-mail them to me."

"Easier said than done. I have no access to the Internet."

"Okay, fax them to me."

"I'll have to track down a machine first."

Miriam muttered an oath. "My God, you are on the dark side of the moon."

"Basically. Just sit tight for a few more days and I'll have a better picture of what's going on."

"It goes without saying that you'll stay there and cover the story as it unfolds."

"You couldn't drag me off this island." She promised to call with the next update, and hung up.

Tara rose. A nervous energy flowed through her body as it did each time she hit on a great story. She went to her bag and dressed in the yoga pants and T-shirt she'd brought. She checked her watch and realized it was only six in the evening.

She ran her fingers through her hair and found her gaze settling on the door that connected to the room next to hers. Kirkland's room.

Curious, she moved to the door and leaned her ear against it. She could hear the deep timbre of his voice and she guessed he was talking to someone at the state or the Boston police department. He hung up. She heard him pacing. His phone rang again and he snapped it up immediately.

Desire curled in her belly and radiated through her body. The warmth spreading through her body pushed out all thoughts that didn't have to do with Kirkland. Closing her eyes, she imagined him wearing a motel towel wrapped around his narrow waist, his chest glistening with the mist from the shower.

Her eyes snapped open and she pulled back from the door and ran tense fingers through her damp hair. "I'm losing my mind."

This potent sexual desire in her had to be borne out of the story. Endorphins always flowed when she landed a scoop, and in the midst of building the story she became edgy and restless. "It's just the story. It's just the story."

But it wasn't *just* the story.

The reality was that she wanted Kirkland. She had since the moment she'd first seen him.

A knock on her door had her flinching. She moved toward it. "Who is it?"

"Kirkland."

Her stomach tightened and she was almost afraid to answer the door. In her current state of mind, who knew what she'd do if she was close enough to touch him?

She moistened her lips. "What do you want?"

"Open the door and you will see." His voice possessed a playfulness she'd never heard before.

Tara laid her hand on the door. She could rattle off six reasons why she should keep her distance from Kirkland. Making a play for him had no upside. Even if she could forget his blue-blood roots, sleeping with him was still a bad idea. Sex between them could compromise the story and her job.

"Tara," he said. His voice had a rusty quality that made her knees weak. "Open the door."

Closing her eyes, Tara touched her hand to the door. She knew what was going to happen if she was alone with Kirkland tonight. She knew they'd end up in her bed.

Keep your distance. Keep your distance.

The chant fell on deaf ears. She released a sigh and opened the door.

Chapter 14

Thursday, July 17, 7:00 p.m.

Tara found Alex standing in the breezeway with a bag of takeout. He had showered but instead of a towel, wore faded jeans and a well-worn, blue Boston Police Department T-shirt.

"Figured we both could use something to eat," he said, holding up the bag.

We. Alarm bells sounded even louder in her head, warning her to refuse. Instead of listening, she mentally shooed them away and opened the door wider. "I'm starving."

He grinned and slid past her into the room. "I was hoping your room had some kind of table."

"Just the bed."

He stared at the bed, now covered with her notes and papers. "Right."

Tara closed the door and crossed the room to her bed. She cleared away her article notes, closed up her laptop and set them all on the dresser by the TV.

"I guess I don't have to guess what you've been working on," he said.

Unapologetic, she shrugged. "I'm working on the article. And I've also been in touch with my editor about it. She's ready to run with the piece as soon as I can file it."

He accepted the information with a nod. "That would explain why your line was busy."

"You called?"

"About dinner."

"Ah."

He set the bag down on the edge of the bed and started to unpack cartons. The smells of marinara and fresh bread made her stomach growl. "State police called and they're still knee-deep in evidence collection at this point. Once this storm passes I'll head back up there."

"I'll be there, too."

He removed plastic forks, napkins and paper plates. "I'd be shocked if you weren't there."

"You're not like most cops."

That had him raising his eyebrow. "Meaning?"

She moved to the end of the bed and sat down, careful to keep a few feet of distance between them. "They are intimidated by my work. They resent me and they certainly don't trust me."

His gaze took on a new intensity. "Should they trust you?"

She raised her chin a fraction. "I'm tenacious and will do what it takes to get the story. But if I give my word, I keep it. Period."

"So if I asked you to sit on a story, you would?"

"If I promised, sure. But generally I don't make that sort of promise."

He nodded as he opened several cartons. "That's fair enough." He handed her a plate and fork. "I wasn't sure what you would like so I settled on Italian."

"I have a cast-iron stomach and can eat anything."

"You should have been a cop." He opened a tinfoil container filled with pasta. "Dig in."

She spooned some spaghetti onto her plate. "Where'd you get this?"

"At the tavern. I persuaded the cook to box us up some dinner."

"I didn't think they'd do that."

He accepted the carton from her and dumped some pasta on his plate. "You have to know how to ask."

She shook her head. "I think Flo likes you better than she does me."

He grinned as if a memory had popped into his head. "You can be brutally direct."

"True." Of course, if she were to be direct now she'd tell Kirkland how much she wanted him. She ached to touch his warm skin and to kiss him. Instead of saying what was on her mind, she took a bite of the pasta. It wasn't bad and she realized that she was hungry. When they'd finished, she collected his plate. "Seeing that you cooked, I'll do the dishes." She dumped the plates and empty cartons in the trash can. "All done."

"You're not the domestic sort, are you?"

She leaned against the bureau by the TV. "Roxie is the queen of frozen and canned food. In fact, we used to joke that if someone took the can opener we'd starve. But I am a great cook. If you tell anyone I will deny it."

He leaned back on his elbows. "I can't picture you in a kitchen."

"Nothing soothes my nerves better than making crème brûlée or flourless chocolate torte."

"You never cease to amaze me."

"I try."

"So what brought you back to Boston? Or better, what took you to D.C.?"

She was more comfortable asking the questions than answering them. "I went because there was a job at the *Washington Post.* It didn't pay much but it was a chance."

"And you couldn't find that closer to home?"

"At the time, I wanted to get away from Boston. I was feeling a little confined after my breakup with Robert." There was no sense in holding back. "I didn't fit in Robert's world—his mother made that very clear to me. But I also didn't feel like I fit in Roxie's world. I just needed a fresh start."

His expression darkened. "If it's worth anything, he'd have made you miserable."

"I know that now."

He rose as if unable to stay away from her any longer. His gaze had darkened, and he possessed a different kind of energy that had her mouth going dry. She moistened her lips.

"I didn't come here to just share dinner with you, Mackey."

Her heartbeat filled her ears and her stomach fluttered. "Really?"

Kirkland moved toward her a step. "I've not been able to get you out of my mind for a long while. Those crisp white shirts of yours have been driving me crazy for almost a year."

Her body tingled. "A whole year? I thought you didn't like me at first."

"I have always noticed you, Mackey. Always. I

started liking you when you agreed to aid in that investigation a few months ago."

"Really?" She moved a step toward him, and he was so close now she could feel the heat of his body.

"I've always noticed your killer figure. But after that case, I couldn't stop thinking about you."

She traced one of the buttons on his shirt with her fingertip. "I have to admit I've had a few thoughts about you."

His eyes brightened with interest. "What kind of thoughts?"

"Very unprofessional thoughts."

He brushed her hair from her shoulder, exposing the soft skin of her neck. Gently he traced the line of her jaw with his thumb. "Such as?"

The idea of voicing the dreams she'd had about Kirkland made her blush. There was no way she could speak of them. But she could show him.

Tara wrapped her arms around Kirkland's neck and raised up on tiptoes to kiss him. He bent his head as he pulled her against him. He tasted so good, and the feel of his hard body against hers sent shivers down her spine.

In the back of her mind, again logic screamed that this was a mistake. And again she ignored it.

Kirkland deepened the kiss, coaxing her lips open with his mouth. He probed the inside of her mouth, exploring, and made her crave his touch with a ferocity that stunned her.

She unfastened the buttons of his shirt. And slowly she slid her hands under the brushed cotton and felt his hard abdominal muscles. He flinched at her touch as if he'd been burned. A low growl rumbled in his chest and he hugged her tighter. She savored the effect she had on him.

He backed her up toward the bed. Together, they sat on the edge. Desire pounded in her veins.

Kirkland kissed her again. His tongue caressed the inside of her mouth as his hand pressed into the small of her back and then slid below her panty line. He cupped her buttocks.

She squirmed, savoring the luscious agony.

Her hands slid down his flat belly and she unfastened the button of his pants. Her hand slid deeper.

"Don't rush this," he warned.

He pushed her back and his hand slid up under her shirt. As he kissed her, his hand slid over her naked breast and teased her nipple into a hard peak.

Tara arched, pressing into his body. "You are driving me nuts."

A chuckle rumbled in his chest. "Good."

"We are about to cross a line," she said, breathless. "The line separates professional and personal."

His hand stilled. "Is that a problem?"

"Not for me. I'm going to write my story regardless of what's happening here."

"I know."

She wanted to be straight with him but it was hard to think clearly. "So we understand each other?"

"Outside...tomorrow...it's about our jobs. Now... it's just us."

"Yes. Just us."

Kirkland's hand slid to the waistband of her sweats and slipped under the soft fabric. He teased her tender flesh. She moaned and arched into his hand.

Tara reached for the waistband and slid her pants off. Kirkland stared down at her naked flesh, his gaze hot with desire. He stood and removed his clothes and she pulled off her T-shirt. Within seconds they were in the middle of the bed. He lay on top of her and they were kissing.

Tara lost track of time as Kirkland kissed and stroked her body. Several times he brought her to the brink and several times he pulled back. She was so moist, so eager for release that she couldn't wait anymore.

She opened her legs and guided him to her entrance. Kirkland needed no more coaxing and she realized that it was taking extreme control for him to hold back. He pushed into her. He filled her to the point of pain. And for a moment she paused as her body became accustomed. He sensed her unease and didn't move inside of her.

"It's been a while for you," he said against her ear.

Nine years. Since Robert. "Yeah."

As she grew accustomed to him, he began to move very slowly in her. Pleasure started to build and soon he fit inside her as if they'd been made to make love.

And then like tinder to kindling, the intensity of their lovemaking exploded. He started to move faster and faster and she found herself spiraling out of control. When she could stand it no more, she arched back and called out his name.

He pushed into her with one final thrust and together they found release.

Kirkland collapsed on top of her. The sweat of their bodies and their rapid heartbeats mingled as they lay in utter contentment.

He rolled on his side, pulling her against him. Her bottom nestled against him. He nestled his chin in the crook of her neck and kissed her on the ear.

Together they drifted off to sleep as the rain pattered above their heads.

Outside a lone figure stood in the rain, staring up at the dark lights of Tara's hotel room. The figure held the loaded .45 in hand and waited for Kirkland to leave Tara Mackey's room.

The reporter had done her job. She'd found Kit.

But now Mackey's tenacious reputation had

become a liability. If not stopped, Mackey would keep digging into the murders of Kit and her driver.

And that couldn't happen.

As the minutes passed and the rain came down harder, it was clear that Kirkland wasn't going to leave her room tonight.

It wasn't a surprise that the reporter was a slut. All those brassy, pushy women like Kit and Tara were whores.

None deserved to live.

Now that Tara had done her job she would die.

Killing Tara Mackey tonight would be out of the question. But soon the opportunity would come and the bitch reporter would die.

Chapter 15

Friday, July 18, 7:00 a.m.

They made love twice more during the night. And in the predawn hours, as the wind and rain had howled outside, Tara had been wrapped in Alex's arms. She had never felt more at peace. This was where she belonged.

As the sun rose, Tara lay on her side. Alex's arm was wrapped possessively around her narrow waist.

She opened her eyes and glanced toward the window. Bright sunlight peeked through the edges of the vinyl curtain. The rain must have stopped.

Like it or not, the cocoon of rain that had shut the outside world out had passed and they both had to face the day.

They had jobs to do.

Last night, her feelings for Alex had seemed crystal-clear, but now, as her mind tripped to reality, she wasn't so sure. After all, what kind of future did they have? They were from very different social worlds. She was often his adversary at work. They always ended up arguing.

Sleeping with Boston's lead homicide detective had not been a wise move. She'd sensed that last night but had not cared.

Cautiously, she tried to lift his arm.

Alex tightened his hold. "Where are you going?" His voice sounded rough, sexy.

"The rain is gone. We can get back up to the cottage."

He sighed and kissed her on the neck. "I don't want to leave this bed ever again."

"We have to get up there. Who knows what Patterson might have discovered?" His hard thighs rubbed against her leg and she felt her resolve waning.

He kissed her on her neck and then rolled her on her back. His hand slid to her breast and he teased her nipple until it was a hard peak. She grew moist as his erection pressed against her.

She opened her legs. She wanted to make love to him one last time. The world could wait another hour.

Alex pushed into her and as she accepted all of him, she wrapped her legs around his hips. His breathing grew faster and he moved inside of her. A spasm rolled over her body, jolting her. He sensed her release and drove harder as he found his own. He collapsed against her. Their sweat mingled.

He nuzzled his bearded chin against her arm. "My God, woman, you are going to kill me."

Her heart hammered against his chest. She chuckled softly.

For a dozen minutes they lay on their sides, their bodies spooned together. They drifted off to sleep and didn't wake until almost eight.

Tara started awake. "Alex, we have to get up."

"You called me Alex."

She blushed. "It's your name."

"Yeah." He kissed her on the neck again. "You're right. We do need to get going. I have to get up to the crime scene." He kissed her on the arm and pushed himself into a sitting position.

She hugged the sheet over her bare breasts as she sat up and leaned against the headboard. The morning air felt cool against her skin. She searched the floor for her T-shirt and sweats. "Whose fault was that?"

He chuckled and traced his finger over the bare skin above the sheet. "I'd say we're both guilty as charged."

She remembered their lovemaking, and heat rose in her cheeks. Spotting her clothes in a puddle on the floor, she slid out from under the sheets and grabbed them.

Alex lay back on the pillow and tucked his hands behind his head. He stared at her naked body, boldly savoring every inch of her. "Where are you off to?"

"To get coffee."

"We could take a shower first." His thick, mussed-up hair combined with his unshaven face made him look almost boyish. Gone were the frown lines from his forehead that normally furrowed so deep.

She shoved the wild tangle of hair out of her eyes. "We will never get out of here if we do."

He shrugged. "That wouldn't be so bad."

Tara shook her head as she slipped on her sweats and pulled her T-shirt over her naked breasts. "I've never seen you this playful. Before you seemed so grim, all business."

His muscled leg jutted out from the sheet. From this angle his scar was plainly visible. "I'm starting to figure out that life's too short."

She felt an emotional shift, a softening in him. And it made her nervous. She'd told Kirkland two days ago she didn't do casual, but honesty and seriousness terrified her. Opening up to him equaled an emotional risk that she sensed would be far deeper than anything she'd shared with Robert.

The risk of getting hurt was far greater than she'd ever anticipated.

"I better get that coffee," she said.

He frowned. "Did I say something wrong?"

"No, no." Where were her damn shoes? She spotted them under the bed and slid them on. "I just really need some coffee." She managed a bright smile and grabbed her wallet. "I'll be back in a few minutes."

Before he could respond she was out the door. In the cool morning, she took in a deep breath, trying to ease the sudden tightening in her chest. What the devil was wrong with her? All the guy had said was that life was too short.

She moved down the breezeway, realizing she knew exactly what was wrong. She was falling in love with Kirkland. *Love*. Damn. Loving him was the last thing she'd expected or wanted.

She went into the tavern and ordered two large coffees to go. She also snagged a couple of bagels with cream cheese, and then headed back up to the room.

When she pushed open the door, steam poured out of the tiny bathroom. Alex was in the shower. Grateful for an extra moment alone, she added sweetener to her coffee and sipped it.

The shower shut off. "Tara, is that you?"

Hearing him call her Tara felt odd. "Yep, it's me. How do you take your coffee? I wasn't sure, so I grabbed everything."

"Black's fine." He emerged from the bath, his lean body wrapped in a towel. Yesterday she'd fantasized about that body and realized the dream paled in comparison to the reality. His body was well muscled and trim.

She moistened her lips and handed him his coffee. "Coffee. Black."

His fingers brushed hers and he leaned over and kissed her on the cheek. "Thanks."

"Coffee practically runs in my veins. I can't live without it."

He brushed back his damp hair with his fingers. "You're one of the few reporters I know who can drink that swill Brady makes. You really do have a cast iron stomach."

"I do. And Brady's java isn't too bad. A bit strong, but manageable. I picked up a couple of bagels and some cream cheese."

He dug a bagel out of the bag and unwrapped the wax paper. "So you mentioned you're a good cook. Somehow I just didn't figure you for the Betty Crocker type."

She shrugged. "If a woman wants to eat well, she learns to cook."

"Something I never would have guessed about you."

"Live and learn."

She dug a hand through her hair. She'd never been one to dodge a touchy subject and she wasn't about to now. "This easy banter between us feels weird. We've never talked like this before."

"We'd never made love before either."

She swallowed. "Right."

His gaze bored into her. "Does this bother you?"

She nodded. "Yeah, a little. When we talk about crime stats, murders or headlines, it feels safe to me. We're colleagues, associates even. But this other stuff...."

"Making love."

"Yeah, and the talk about each other... That is very uncharted territory for me. I've been careful not to get too close to anyone since Robert."

Alex set his coffee and bagel down and moved toward her. He set her coffee beside his and laid his hands on her shoulders. He kissed her gently on the lips. "I'm willing to map a new course if you are."

Tara's stomach fluttered with nervous anticipation. "You mean like dating?"

He shrugged. "Why not? You have dated before haven't you?"

"Well, not exactly. Not since Robert." She shrugged. "I've got lots of guy friends but it's never gotten to the stage we reached last night."

"Wow."

She felt strangely embarrassed that she'd lived like a nun for so long. "Yeah."

He traced her collarbone with his thumb. "But I

hear dating is like riding a bike. Once you learn, you never forget."

"In this room, being with you doesn't seem all that difficult. Out there," she said, nodding to the window, "I'm afraid it might be a different story. Life just has a way of getting in the way."

He frowned. "Life?"

"We are kind of an odd couple, don't you think? Backgrounds, jobs, families." She drew in a breath and let it out slowly. "I don't want to put the cart before the horse but I don't want to get involved with a guy whose family won't accept me." There. She'd said it.

"Tara, look at me, and my life choices. I haven't listened to my family in a long, long time."

"Maybe as far as your career is concerned you've done your own thing. But I've learned people pay more attention to family and tradition when it comes to more personal matters."

"Tara, I married the perfect woman. Or so my family and friends kept telling me. It was a disaster."

"You looked pretty chummy with Regina at the club." She couldn't hide the hint of jealousy. It was hard not to compare herself to Regina. But she'd never possess Regina's cool, smooth looks and the calm sophistication that came with years of breeding.

He smiled. "Regina doesn't love me and, in fact, I doubt she ever did. She was in love with my money and position. And she hates to lose. My walking away from the marriage constituted a big loss." He brushed the hair away from her shoulder.

She tilted her head forward into his chest.

He cupped her face in his hands and tipped her face up so her gaze met his. "I'd like to give us a shot."

"Rationally, I know I'm overthinking this. I do a lot of that."

"It's one of your quirks that I like."

"Give it time. I'll drive you nuts."

He laughed and kissed her. She wrapped her arms around his neck. Alex's cell phone rang. He ignored it.

Tara was honestly grateful for the interruption. "The outside world calls, Detective."

He continued to ignore it. "Do you want to give us a try?"

"I suppose."

He looked amused. "That was hardly a ringing endorsement."

It did sound lame. "Sorry, I'm just wondering how much to invest in you. I don't want to get burned."

The phone stopped ringing. "I guess neither one of us can predict the future. But I can promise that I'd never willingly hurt you."

"But unwillingly you might. Boy, you know just the right things to say."

His phone started to ring again. This time he couldn't ignore it. He kissed her and moved away toward his clothes, which were dangling from the edge of the bed. He unhooked the phone from the belt holster and snapped it open. "Kirkland."

As he listened to the caller, he propped the phone under his ear, pulled his towel away and reached for his pants. Her gaze was drawn to a long, angry scar that ran down his right hip and leg. It was a harsh reminder of the dangers of his job.

"Thanks for the update, Patterson," Alex said. "I'll be up at the cottage in a half hour."

The outside world had found them. He closed the phone. "That was Patterson. He's got something up at the cottage he wants us to see."

Oddly, she felt relief. Crime was more predictable than love.

Alex wound his car up the coastal road, trying to find a way to tell Tara that he really cared about her without scaring her off. Clearly, her relationship with Stanford had left a lasting mark on her, and she was quite skittish when it came to commitment.

She'd pulled her hair back again in a tight ponytail and donned a fresh shirt to go with her slacks. She was all business.

He realized Tara wasn't so different from him. She didn't put much stock in words and promises. She judged people by actions and deeds. He'd have to find a way to *show* her that he cared and that he had no intention of going anywhere.

He parked his car behind a state police cruiser. Yellow crime-scene tape around the entrance of the cottage drooped from last night's rain. There must have been twenty cops here now, canvassing the surrounding area.

Alex and Tara got out of the car. She grabbed her camcorder from the backseat and immediately started filming.

Before he could warn her to stop, Patterson's sharp voice cut through the crowd. "Shut that off, Ms. Mackey, or I'll have you escorted back to town."

She kept filming. "I have every right to cover this crime scene."

Patterson moved in front of her camera. Dark circles hung under the detective's eyes and Alex guessed the guy had been up here all night. "And I can't do my job if a reporter starts leaking information to the public."

"I'll just take exterior shots," she argued.

Mackey had argued with Kirkland countless times over similar issues. "Tara, put the camera away. Let Patterson do his job. We all want this crime solved."

She lowered the camera. "Fine."

Patterson extended his hand to Alex. They shook. "Detective Kirkland, I'd like for you to come inside. There's something I want to show you."

"Sure." He started inside. Tara started to follow.

Patterson frowned. "Nice try. You stay outside."

Tara planted her hands on her hips. "Hey, if it wasn't for me you guys wouldn't have a case."

Alex sympathized with Tara. She had picked up this case when it had gone cold. "Patterson is right. This is no place for reporters. Not now."

Fire jumped from Tara's gaze. "It's my story."

"It's my murder investigation," Patterson said.

Tara drew in a deep breath. "What if I said that I won't report anything I see inside until you give the all clear? I give you my word that this will be strictly off the record."

She'd said last night that her word meant everything to her. And Kirkland had believed her. There'd been a few times he'd asked her to keep quiet on the details of a murder and she had. "It's not up to me, it's up to Patterson." He faced the other officer.

Patterson looked at him as if he were crazy. "She will blab the first second she gets."

"Hey, sport," Tara said, directing her comments at Patterson. The rush of color in her face was a sign that she was losing her temper. "This isn't the elementary-school playground. And we aren't whispering about Susie and Johnny kissing behind the swing set. I get that this needs to stay quiet. I can keep my mouth shut."

Patterson set his jaw.

"I can vouch for her," Alex said.

Patterson shot him a glance. "Kirkland has a good

rep, so if he vouches for you, I'll allow it. But if one word of this gets leaked, it's your hide, Mackey."

She didn't flinch. "Agreed."

Patterson nodded and the trio walked inside the house. Now that the storm had passed, sunlight streamed through the windows. While the house had been dark and gloomy yesterday, today it was almost cheery. Out the north window was a clear view of the ocean.

"The place looks completely different during the day," Tara said. "I can almost see why Kit picked it."

Alex still couldn't picture the sophisticated Kit living here. "I don't think aesthetics had anything to do with her choosing this place. She had a reason for being here."

"You're right," Patterson said. "She had a very good reason for being here."

Chapter 16

Friday, July 18, 10:00 a.m.

Tara could barely contain her curiosity. "So out with it, Patterson. Why was Kit here?"

The state police officer shot her a glance that told her he didn't like her one bit. So she shot him back another glance that told him she didn't care one bit.

Patterson cleared his throat. "It seems Kit was running a computer-scam operation out of her house. She's got a satellite hookup outside as well as solar panels. As long as the sun is shining she's got the solar juice to power her operation."

Tara wasn't shocked. "That certainly fits Brenda's MO."

Patterson rubbed the back of his neck with his hand. "For the sake of clarity, can we stick to one name? Kit, Brenda, Bess. Pick any one."

"Kit," Tara said. "It's how most know her."

Patterson nodded. "It seems *Kit* was busy setting up her scams within a month of arriving here. Her computer records are chock-full of stings."

Alex studied the computer. "Patterson, mind if I poke around?"

"Help yourself."

Alex sat down at the computer and started opening several programs. "She's made almost a million."

"And it all is stored offshore in the Cayman Islands," Patterson said.

"Which means," Tara added, "whoever has the account and password has access to the money. Is that information missing?"

Admiration flickered in Patterson's eyes. "No, it's not. The access numbers were all on her Rolodex. It wouldn't have taken much to find them. Whoever killed Kit didn't want the passwords."

Alex rubbed the back of his neck. "Robinson's place was ransacked. All the gems were taken. I'd say robbery was a motive behind that killing."

Patterson nodded. "The gems found on Borelli match the inventory taken from the jeweler's store. I think Borelli killed Robinson, took the gems and then came up here."

"The question is, who shot Borelli and Kit?" Tara said as she watched Alex expertly maneuver through the computer programs.

Alex studied the screen. "It looks like Kit was working with someone in Boston."

"Could she have been working with her former chauffeur?" Tara asked. "There were rumors in Boston that they were lovers. Maybe that's true."

Patterson shrugged. "I don't know. Kit didn't have any personal items here at the cottage that would link her to the past. I can tell you that she had two airline tickets dated for the tenth of next month. She was planning to leave for Fiji."

"Why didn't she leave the country earlier?" Tara said. "She could have taken off a year ago."

"I can answer that one. Borelli wouldn't have been able to get a passport until just recently because he was on parole for a felony drug violation. With no more probation hanging over him, he would have been free to leave the country."

"So Kit waited for him?" Tara asked.

Alex shrugged. "Seems so."

"Was Borelli his legal name?" Tara asked as another possibility occurred to her.

"No," Alex said. "It was Martin."

Tara snapped her fingers. She pulled a notebook

out of her camera bag and started to flip through her notes from the other day. She tapped her finger against an entry. "Mrs. Shoemaker mentioned a half brother. His last name was Martin."

Alex's eyes narrowed. "Borelli and Kit were brother and sister."

"Did you find the gems Kit was wearing the day she married Landover?" Tara asked.

Patterson shook his head. "No. If they'd been in the sack Borelli had on him, then they were taken."

"How much of this place have you searched?" Alex asked.

"Not much," Patterson admitted. "But we're going to take the place apart."

Tara's mind reeled through the facts. Borelli and Kit were siblings. "I'll bet money that whoever sent me the information on the Kit/Brenda connection knew Borelli was her brother. Whoever sent me that information set me up. They wanted me to find Kit so that they could follow me and kill her." She thought about the night her motel door had rattled. It wasn't a case of a confused guest. Someone had been trying to get into her room. "I just can't figure how Robinson fits into all this."

Alex leaned back in the chair. "Robinson had a past including felony convictions for theft."

"Do you think the three were working together?" Kit asked.

"Very possible," Alex said. "Kit would need someone like Robinson to help her fence such easily identified gems."

"Do we know how the killer got onto the island?" Tara asked.

Patterson shoved his hands in his pockets and rattled the loose change. "My men have started interviewing people and so far no one has seen anyone out of the ordinary."

"Miller's Cove is a mile from town," Tara said. "I'll bet the killer came in by private boat and walked into town."

Alex nodded. "And then made the eight-mile trek up a rocky road at night and then turned around and walked back. That's twenty miles to cover."

Tara smiled. "The killer didn't walk up the mountain." She loved it when the pieces of a puzzle came together. "The killer drove Florence's car."

"You're losing me," Patterson said.

Alex reached for his cell. He understood where she was going with this. "Florence is a waitress in town. She thought her son had banged up the front bumper and she was angry at him because he denied it."

"The killer drove up the mountain road at night and hit the pile of rocks we almost hit while we headed up here the next morning," Tara continued.

Alex shoved out a breath. "Patterson, you better

get your forensics team into town to check out that truck. It might have the only bit of trace evidence left of our killer."

Two hours later, Tara watched a distraught Florence arguing with Patterson as his men dusted her truck for fingerprints. The entire inside was covered with black dusting powder. The police had lifted a lot of prints but it could take days to determine who they belonged to.

Many of the folks from town had gathered and were discussing this latest turn of events. No one had ever been murdered in Sable Point and now the town had seen two murders.

Tara spoke to several people about Kit, the woman they knew as Bess. She'd collected a handful of stories, and from what she'd been able to piece together, Bess only came into town for supplies. She liked magazines, especially about movie stars, and she favored chocolate. She didn't mix with people at all and always wore a hat and sunglasses.

The cops hadn't roped Miller's Cove off yet and Tara knew if she didn't sneak a look soon, she'd never get the chance. While Alex spoke to Patterson, Tara drove over to the cove on the narrow dirt road.

When she reached the end of the road, she grabbed her camera and started down the rocky path that led to the tiny beach. Halfway down, she slipped on a jagged rock and nearly dropped her camera. Muttering an oath, she glanced at the raw skin at her ankle before moving onto the dock.

She snapped a couple dozen pictures from all angles and then, seeing nothing else of interest, returned to town.

Kit, Borelli and Robinson—all three had criminal backgrounds and reinvented lives, and they'd all lived in Boston at the same time and had moved in the same circles.

Tara was beginning to believe that the answers to these murders were back in Boston.

Chapter 17

Friday, July 18, 5:00 p.m.

Tara followed Alex in her car all the way from Sable Point into Boston. They'd not stopped during the four-hour ride but as they approached the city her cell phone rang.

She flipped it open. "Mackey."

"It's Alex."

On the island she'd felt so connected to him but as they got closer and closer to the city she started to feel as though she was losing the connection they'd shared. When she and Robert had met at college everything had been fine. It was only when they'd returned to Boston that the trouble had started.

"Hey."

"I've got to head into work. I'll call you later."

I'll call you later. There was a loaded line. "Sure."

"I will call," he added, as if he'd sensed something in her voice.

"I know. Hey, my exit is coming up. I've got to go."

"Okay."

She hung up. All she wanted now was to find Roxie and talk to her. She needed Roxie to banish her fears and tell her she was worrying over nothing.

Tara pushed through the doors of the bar just after five o'clock. The place was busy and Roxie was behind the bar, serving drinks. One glance told Tara tonight was going to be a packed one so she quickly changed into jeans and put on her apron. Twenty minutes after arriving home she was waiting tables.

It was too hectic for her to talk to Roxie but a couple of times she caught her aunt staring at her. Roxie knew her better than anyone and she'd likely guessed that something more had happened while Tara was gone.

At ten-fifteen, Tara moved toward the table of new arrivals. They were all sleekly dressed women who clearly didn't fit in this part of town. Tara recognized Regina instantly. The woman stared up at her with the contented smile of a cat ready to eat a mouse.

Tara plastered on her best smile. “Welcome to Roxie’s.”

Three of the women didn’t even bother to glance in her direction. But Regina’s grin broadened. “Tara? What on earth are you doing here?”

“I work here,” she said matter-of-factly.

“But I thought you were a reporter.”

Tara shrugged. Regina wasn’t fooling anyone. She knew exactly what she was doing. “I’ve got bills to pay, like most, and the extra money helps.”

Regina tried to suppress a giggle, as if a second job were something to be embarrassed about. “Oh, right, sure.”

Tara didn’t feel the least bit of shame. She had student loans to pay and an aunt to help. Period. “So what can I get you ladies?”

Regina tossed a glance at her friends. “Four white wines. The best you have.”

“Sure.” As she moved to the bar, Roxie caught her gaze.

Roxie lifted a plucked eyebrow. “So what do the snooty-dos want?”

“Four wines.” And then, mimicking Regina, she said, “Your best.”

Roxie pulled a jug bottle with a twist top from under the bar and started to fill four glasses. “What are they doing here?”

Tara grabbed a handful of peanuts from the bar

and popped them in her mouth. She'd not eaten since lunch. "Who knows? But I'm flashing back to junior high when Missy Bevins told me to stay away from Wally Cantrell."

Roxie set the wineglasses on Tara's tray. "You lost me there, kid."

"Regina is Alex's ex-wife. Regina has figured out that Alex might have a thing for me."

Roxie's eyes glinted. "A thing between you and Detective Good-Looking? Is it a good thing?"

"It was while we were on Sable Point. We'll see if it lasts." She didn't sound hopeful because she didn't want it to fall apart. She didn't want to get hurt again.

"Kirkland ain't no Robert, honey. He's a man who doesn't back away from what he wants."

Tara wished she had the same conviction. Alex hadn't called her since her return and it was bothering her more than she'd ever admit. "I know."

Roxie reached for Tara's tray. "Why don't you let me deliver their drinks? I'd like to get a gander at the ex."

Tara smiled. "Thanks, but I can handle Regina and her buddies."

Roxie leaned forward. "Doll, I've run interference for you since you were a peanut. I don't mind doing it tonight."

"Thanks. But this is something I have to do."

Roxie twirled her finger around her large gold hoop

earring. "Expect the snooty-dos to hate what you put in front of them. They didn't come here to have a drink."

"I figured as much." She hoisted the tray and headed to Regina's table. She served the drinks. "Is there anything else I can get you?"

Regina took a sip of her wine. She wrinkled her nose. "This is the best you have?"

Tara shrugged. "Sure is."

Regina set her glass down and glanced at her friends, who all looked as if they'd just tasted something awful. "It's not acceptable."

"Why are you here?" Tara asked. Her feet hurt, her back ached and she still had a couple of hours of work to do on her article. She had no patience for games tonight. "This isn't your part of town and this isn't your kind of place."

Regina's eyes hardened. "You are direct."

Tara arched an eyebrow, waiting for Regina's response to her original question.

Regina rose and her friends followed. Her eyes had darkened with anger. "All right, if you want to be direct then I can be direct as well. Alex might be having a bit of fun with you now, but he will get bored with you. He belongs with me, not you."

Tara didn't flinch but she felt the sting of the barb. "You drove across town to tell me that? Well, great. Consider your message delivered." She held out her palm. "That'll be twenty bucks for the wine."

Regina raised her chin. "I'm not paying anything. The wine was undrinkable."

Tara's gaze didn't waver. And then, in a voice loud enough for all to hear, she said, "Roxie, call the cops. We have a few deadbeats."

Regina's lips flattened. "How dare you?"

"You ordered the wines and now you will pay for them or I report you all."

"You are so common." Regina snapped open her purse and pulled out a twenty. She tossed it on the table.

The women stalked out but Tara felt no sense of victory. She snapped up the bill and collected the untouched wine.

Regina had hit the heart of Tara's insecurities just as Missy had when she'd called Tara a bastard in front of Mrs. Young's sixth grade class. Tara cursed herself for being so insecure or for caring that anyone would think she wasn't good enough.

"Let it go," she muttered as she headed back to work.

By the time Tara ushered the last customer out the door it was past midnight and she was so tired she could barely see straight.

Roxie locked the front door as Tara cleared the last of the dishes off the tables. "Anything else you want to tell me about the good detective?"

"Maybe another day."

Roxie snapped her fingers and began to fish under the bar. She dug out a brown manila envelope. "I almost forgot. You got an envelope this afternoon."

Tara opened the envelope. "It's from Pierce. He wants to meet."

Chapter 18

Saturday, July 19, 9:00 a.m.

Tara had never been one to wait around for a man to call. If she wanted to talk to him, she called. But for some reason this morning as she got dressed for her meeting with Pierce, she couldn't summon the courage to call Alex. In fact as each minute passed, the time they'd spent together on that island seemed more and more distant, as if it had never happened.

Tara ran a brush through her red hair and pulled it back into a tight ponytail. She slid on the navy blue tailored jacket that matched neatly creased pants.

She checked her watch, and knew she had plenty of time to have a cup of coffee and scan her notes. The more she thought about this story the more she believed that the key lay with the gems. Tara also believed they hadn't been sold. Kit's secret bank account had a balance of just under a million, and if the gems had been sold the balance would be higher. Of course, she could have stashed the money elsewhere, but Tara's gut told her Kit hadn't sold them yet. Kit, Borelli and Robinson—her gut told her the trio had been working together. They'd somehow come up with a scheme to steal the Landover gems.

She swallowed the rest of her coffee and decided to head out even though she was still running early. Better to be thirty minutes early than late.

The drive across town was easy, and she had no trouble finding a parking spot. Things rarely went this well, and she decided it had to be a sign she was meant to talk to Pierce.

At five minutes to eleven, she knocked on the front door. This time Mrs. Reston answered the door. The woman's face was stern and held not the least bit of welcome. "Ms. Mackey."

Tara nodded, refusing to let the woman's icy stare make her feel inferior. "I'm here for Mr. Landover."

Mrs. Reston stepped back and opened the door wider. "He's expecting you in his study upstairs."

Tara moved inside. "Thanks."

The woman closed the door behind her. "Detective Kirkland was here last night. He told Mr. Landover about Kit."

It made sense that Alex would be the one to deliver the news. "I hope Mr. Landover will be all right."

"He's a brave man and he would never show his true emotions. But I can tell he's devastated."

"I'm sorry."

"You're not sorry. No reporter is sorry when they get their story. You've stirred up trouble and pain that was best left alone."

Tara hadn't expected Mrs. Reston to welcome her but she'd not anticipated this anger, either. "Isn't it better to have the truth?"

"The truth is overrated."

"I'm not here to argue the point with you or apologize that I did my job. I'm here to see Mr. Landover as he requested."

Mrs. Reston's eyes narrowed as she turned and led Tara up carpeted stairs to the second floor. Mrs. Reston knocked on a closed door at the end of the hallway.

"Enter." Pierce's stern voice echoed out from behind the door.

Mrs. Reston opened the door and announced Tara.

"Send her in," he said.

Despite her bravado, butterflies chewed at Tara's stomach as she stepped into the study. Her gaze skimmed past wood-paneled walls, a rich oriental carpet and twin leather chairs to Pierce, who stood behind a richly carved mahogany desk. He was dressed in dark pants and a starched white shirt. Thick gray hair brushed back off his face accentuated the deeply lined but distinguished face.

Behind Tara, Mrs. Reston closed the study door. And for just a moment, Tara flashed back to standing in a similar room ten years ago. The study had belonged to Robert's father and he'd been writing her a check. The generous sum had been offered in exchange for her promise that she drop Robert. She'd told him in plain terms what he could do with the check. The next day, Robert had broken up with her.

She cleared her throat. "Mr. Landover. It's a pleasure."

His expression held no hint of welcome, but there was weariness behind his eyes. "Have a seat."

She moved to one of the plush armchairs, sat and rested her briefcase beside her. From a bag she pulled a handheld recorder. "I'm sorry about your wife."

He sighed. "She's been dead to me for a year. You'd have thought the news Detective Kirkland brought me wouldn't have been painful. But it was."

"I am sorry for your loss."

He nodded.

As much as he must be hurting, she'd come here to interview him at his request. "May I record our interview?"

He sat and folded his hands neatly in front of him. "No. This is strictly off the record."

Off the record. She should have known. "I thought you invited me here so that you could tell me your side of the story."

"I did. I think you've earned the right. But that doesn't mean I think the world deserves to know." The edge of his thin mouth lifted into what some would describe as a smile. "If you don't agree to my terms then there won't be an interview today."

As much as Tara wanted this puzzle solved, she was willing to bet that Pierce wanted his story told more. He had a huge ego and couldn't let this story pass without being included. She rose. "Thank you for your time."

His shock was evident on his face. "You're leaving?"

"On the record is the only way I'll play this."

A heavy silence filled the room as he stared at her. Finally he nodded. "Agreed."

Tara didn't show her relief or joy. Instead she sat back down quietly and turned on her recorder.

"How did you find out about my wife's past? I worked very hard to bury it."

That shocked her. "You knew about her history?"

"Of course. A man in my position needs to know everything about everyone he comes in contact with." He tapped his finger on a file. "I could tell you a few things about you, as well."

She didn't bother glancing at the file. "If that's meant to distract me it doesn't. I'm here to talk about Kit."

He shrugged.

"How did you meet her? The newspapers reported you met at a gala."

"That's what I wanted everyone to believe." He drew in a breath and for a moment lost himself in a pleasant memory. Then he seemed to steel himself. "I met Kit at a party in New York. Her looks caught my attention immediately. The woman could be spellbinding. I asked her to my suite in New York and she came. We spent the night together. When it came time for her to leave, I didn't want her to go. She was stunning, very bright and frankly hypnotic. She was a breath of fresh air to me."

Tara decided to tackle the delicate subject head-on. "She had an arrest record for prostitution in New York. Did she tell you about her past?"

He shook his head. "No. I had her investigated and when I found out the truth I honestly didn't care. I knew with a little time and patience I could remake her into the perfect wife. So I created a new identity for her."

That surprised Tara. "I thought she'd fooled you."

He grinned. "I may be old but I'm not that foolish. I knew what I was getting into when I married her."

"Was it your idea to go to Cadence to mine for the new identity?"

"No. That was hers. She was oddly sentimental

about the town." He leaned back in his chair. "You can see why I don't want this known publicly. I broke a few laws to make her into Kit."

"Did you also engineer her disappearance?"

"No. I was devastated when I thought she'd been murdered."

"Did you know Borelli was her brother?"

"Yes. She loved him and wanted to take care of him. And he was someone I could trust her with."

"When's the last time you saw him?"

"Last year at our wedding. She kissed me on the terrace and said she'd be right back. I never saw her again." He steepled his fingers. "She must have been planning her disappearance for months."

"Why would she leave you on your wedding day? She'd have everything when she married you."

"That's all I thought about last night. All I can think is that she hated Boston. Hated the world I lived in. She wanted me to leave it, but I couldn't. We started arguing before the wedding. I even lost my temper and hit her." He sighed. "As the months passed she grew increasingly bored. She started making comments about breaking up. I reminded her that I'd made her and could destroy her as well. After that, she stopped talking about breaking up. I thought she understood her place and that we'd be fine."

He may have loved Kit but to him she was a possession. "But Kit wasn't really happy, was she?"

"I suppose not."

Tara leaned forward. "Where do you think the gems are?"

Anger and sadness reflected in his pale blue eyes. "I don't know. Whoever has them should know that they were marked by a laser. They are completely traceable."

"So you don't think she sold them."

"Kit knew that the necklace was important to me. It had been in my family for six generations. And it was worth a fortune."

Tara almost felt sorry for him. "Who do you think killed your wife?"

He shook his head as if the energy had drained completely from him. "I don't know. But I want to find out. I owe that to her." He pressed his fingertips to his temple. "I have a headache. This interview is going to have to end."

"One more question?"

"I've given you enough already."

Tara rose and left the room. At the end of the hallway Mrs. Reston waited for her. "What did he want with you?"

Tara kept walking. "You'll have to ask him."

Alex was waiting for Tara when she came out of the Landover home. He'd gone by the bar and Roxie had been happy to tell him where she was.

There were issues that he and Tara needed to resolve between them. Already he felt as if she were drifting away.

She was halfway down the stairs when she spotted him. He noted that her eyes narrowed and her shoulders stiffened just a little. She'd pulled her hair back in a tight ponytail and he found he missed the way it brushed her shoulders when it was loose. "Kirkland."

"So we're back to last names, *Tara?*"

She closed the gap between them. "I like last names. Keeps a bit of distance."

"That's a topic for another day, Tara. Right now I want to ask you about your article."

"What about it?" Her tone became defensive.

"I want you to put it on ice for a while. At least until we can process the information we have from the crime scenes."

She shook her head. "Kirkland, you must be crazy if you think I'm going to sit on this article. I'm going home right now to write it and file it. It should hit the stands in Sunday's paper."

"I would have thought that after what we shared the other day you'd at least try to work with me."

She stiffened as if he'd slapped her. "So was that what the other night was all about? Were you just looking for some kind of emotional hook to control me?"

This wasn't what he'd intended for them to talk about. "No. You're misreading everything."

Tara shook her head. "I doubt it. I think I read it just right." She stormed to her car and got in.

He followed and stared at her through the glass. "Tara, just hold off until I give you the all clear. The more you reveal the harder it will be to catch the killer."

She fired up the engine. "Forget it."

"This is serious. There is a murderer out there. I'm worried about your safety."

"Save it. I'm headed home to write the article now."

It was five o'clock when Tara finished the draft of her article. She could have e-mailed it off to Miriam immediately, but she found herself replaying what Kirkland had said. Could this article compromise his investigation? There was enough doubt for her to hold off sending the e-mail until morning. She'd told him originally that she'd gotten into this because she was looking for justice. Was it justice she wanted or headlines?

She switched off her computer and headed down the stairs to the first-floor bar. Roxie had the night off so it was Tara's job to run the bar. Martha worked the tables while Tara ran the bar and the register. There was little time to think about Alex or the article.

At the end of the night Tara sent Martha home and she was ushering out the last of the customers. She'd not heard from Alex all day and she was sorry now she'd lost her temper. She owed him a phone call first thing in the morning.

She flipped the dead bolt in place and started back toward the bar. A knock at the front door had her pausing. "We're closed," she said, turning in the hopes that it might be Alex at the front door.

It was Cecilia Reston.

Curious, Tara moved to the door and opened it. "What do you want, Mrs. Reston?"

The woman looked tense and had lost a good bit of the poise she had had earlier. "I need to talk to you."

"It's kinda late."

"It's important."

Tara opened the door and stepped aside. When Mrs. Reston was inside Tara closed and locked the door. "What can I do for you?"

"Have you filed your article on Kit yet?"

"No."

She clutched her purse close to her chest. "Good, I'm not too late."

"I'm filing the article in the morning."

Mrs. Reston frowned. "You won't send that article in."

"Yes, I will."

Mrs. Reston tightened her hold on her slim purse.

"Financially, I can make it worth your while if you make it go away."

Tara rubbed her hands over her apron. "I can't do that."

"Money could go a long way to settling debts. I know you have quite a few. It could even help Roxie with the second mortgage she took out on the bar."

Tara frowned. "How do you know about that?"

Mrs. Reston's smile was pleasant but there was steel behind her eyes. "You'd be surprised what I know."

"Maybe it's better you leave."

"I'm not going anywhere."

The hard tone in Mrs. Reston's voice had Tara turning back toward her.

Tara found herself staring into the barrel of a gun.

Alex had spent the better part of the day kicking himself. He and Tara had argued about her stories in the past, hell, he'd even asked her to kill them before, but she'd always done what she thought was best and he respected her for that. And today, he'd used what they'd had to wield influence over her. In short, he'd been an ass.

He downshifted his car and rounded the corner near Roxie's. He wasn't sure what he was going to say to make amends to her. But he'd think of something. Tara was too important to him to lose.

* * *

The pieces fell together for Tara as she stared at Mrs. Reston's gun. It was pointed at her heart now. "You killed them all, didn't you?"

Mrs. Reston flicked the edge of the gun toward one of the booths. "Sit down."

Tara held up her hands as she held her ground. It took all her self-control to keep her voice calm. "We don't need guns, Mrs. Reston."

The older woman shook her head. "I tried to ask nicely. I tried to pay you off. But you refused. You should have taken the money."

Tara's heart hammered in her chest. "Why do you care so much about an article?"

"Because Pierce cannot endure any more scandal. His heart won't take it. He was foolish to talk to you today. I begged him not to but he wouldn't listen. He doesn't quite understand that your story will stir up everything again and we will have to endure months if not years of questions and innuendo. We've only just gotten our lives back to normal."

Tara noted the tension and worry in the woman's voice. "*We*. You keep saying *we*."

"That's right, *we*. Pierce and I have been together for twenty-five years. I've seen him through bad marriages, ungrateful children and the worst problem of them all—Kit Westgate."

Tara's gaze flickered again to the barrel of the

gun. She had no doubt that Mrs. Reston would kill her. There was a manic energy in the woman's eyes that suggested she'd gone over the edge. "I can drop the story if it's that upsetting to you. I didn't realize that what I was doing was so hurtful."

Mrs. Reston's lips curled into a smile that looked more like a snarl. "No, it's too late for that. If you'd shown a little greed earlier then I might, *might* have been able to work with you. Now you're going to have to die."

"Mrs. Reston, if you kill me people will look to you as a suspect sooner or later. They might even blame Mr. Landover."

"Pierce won't be implicated and neither will I. No one is going to find your body."

Tara tried to stay calm. *Keep her talking.* "I promise—I swear—that I will not run that article."

Mrs. Reston backed up. "Stop talking. You're starting to irritate me. Tell me, does Roxie's have gas or electric stoves?"

She swallowed her panic. "Detective Kirkland knows I've written this story. He will come after you."

"He's going to think you died in a fire. He's not going to realize you've been murdered."

"What?"

"Fires start all the time, Ms. Mackey." She smiled sadly. "Sometimes bad things happen to good people."

Tara swallowed. "At least tell me how you found out about Kit." She'd play to her ego. Criminals often believed they were smarter than the rest. "You found out something even the police couldn't figure out. At least give me the satisfaction of knowing how you figured it all out."

Mrs. Reston stared at her and then shrugged. "Why not? I have a moment."

Tara almost sighed with relief. The more time she bought the better her chances of getting away. "How did you find out about Kit's past?"

"Believe it or not it was foolish luck. I guess I can be grateful that there is no honor among thieves."

"I don't understand."

"It was just a week ago. I'd convinced Pierce to let me start clearing out Kit's room. I reasoned she'd been gone a year and wasn't coming back. It was time to give her clothes to charity where they'd do someone some good."

"You really thought she was dead?"

"Honestly, I did. And I was thrilled when all that blood was found. I hated that woman."

Millions in gems, and Tara now realized that passion, not greed, had been behind Kit's death.

Mrs. Reston stood a little straighter. "I assumed one of the men Kit liked to flirt with had killed her. She loved to play with men's affections." She smoothed her hand over her hair. "Be that as it may, she was gone and life was returning to the way it had been before she arrived. As I said, I was cleaning out her room and packing up her clothes. I always check pockets before I send clothes out to clean and so I was checking hers. I found a note in one of her jacket pockets."

"A note? What did it say?"

"It was a letter from some shopgirl in New York. She was demanding hush money from Kit or she'd show Pierce *Brenda's* rap sheet." She shook her head. "Apparently the woman had seen Kit in New York when she'd been there shopping with friends. The woman had worked the streets with Brenda in New York."

"So you realized then that Kit had been a fraud."

"Yes. I just knew she was too good to be true. I knew she had fooled Pierce." She moistened her lips. "I had a private investigator look into Brenda's past. That's when I realized Borelli was her brother." Her eyes narrowed. "I began to wonder if Kit was dead. She'd disappeared once, so why not do it a second time with millions in gems?"

"Did you tell Pierce?"

"Yes. He was furious *with me*. He told me he was aware of his wife's past." She shook her head in disbelief. "He knew she'd been a whore. And he believed she would never fake her death and leave him." Her mouth flattened and tears glistened in her eyes. "He told me to pack my things and get out of his house. He fired me."

A part of Tara almost felt sorry for Mrs. Reston. "You love him very much, don't you?"

A tear rolled down her cheek. "Yes. And I knew I needed to find Kit to make him believe that his precious wife had left him. He needed to realize I was the only one he could trust."

The pieces were falling together. "So you sent Brenda's rapsheet to me."

"You'd been by the house that very morning asking questions. It felt like providence to me. I knew you'd find Kit if you had a little help. You're tenacious."

"Did you run me off the road?"

She shook her head. "No. It was Borelli. I started following him. Your visit scared him." She smiled. "And he did exactly what I'd hoped he'd do. He panicked."

Tara wagered a guess. "He killed Robinson."

"Yes. He went to Robinson demanding the gems. The three had conspired all along to steal them together. Robinson's job was to cut the stones and remove the laser marks. Borelli realized that Robinson had already sold the gems to a private dealer in the Mid East. Borelli shot the jeweler and took all the gems in the store." She smiled. "And then he went running to his sister."

"And you followed him and killed them both."

"She was easy to kill. I shot her in the living room seconds after she opened her door. I must say the look of shock on her face was priceless." Her smile turned hard. "Borelli was harder. He started to run. I chased him to the cliff and shot him. And then he fell."

Tara glanced around the tavern room looking for something she could use to defend herself. "Why do you care if I run this article? It will totally discredit Kit."

"When the police told Pierce last night about finding her body, Pierce came to me and apologized. He begged my forgiveness. He was sorry for all the things he said. He wept in my arms. And I forgave him. I knew I couldn't let this article come out. The poor man had suffered enough. I needed to protect him."

Tara knew if she sat quietly by, Mrs. Reston was going to kill her. She needed to do something. Rising, Tara said, "I won't run the article. I give you my word."

The woman sneered. "Stop repeating yourself. You sound like a fool." She waved her gun. "Now get on the floor and put your hands behind your head."

Tara fisted her fingers. "No."

Mrs. Reston fired her gun.

Alex heard the shot as he approached the tavern. He pulled his weapon. His heart pounding, he crouched and moved toward the picture window. Through the glass he saw Mrs. Reston standing over Tara, who lay on the floor, bleeding. For a heart-stopping moment, he thought he was too late. And then he raised his gun, rushed to the door and kicked it open.

Mrs. Reston whirled around with her gun pointed. He didn't hesitate. He fired, hitting her in the shoulder and knocking her flat.

He ran the distance to Mrs. Reston and kicked the gun far from her reach. He called dispatch, reported the shot and requested an ambulance. As he cuffed Mrs. Reston, distant police sirens wailed.

Alex holstered his weapon and went to Tara. He rolled her on her back. The blood he'd seen was coming from her arm. She was alive.

His voice broke when he spoke. "Tara, can you hear me?"

Her eyes opened. "Where is Mrs. Reston?"

"She's down." He shrugged off his jacket, balled it up and pressed it into Tara's bleeding shoulder.

Tara moistened her lips. "She killed Kit and her brother."

"Okay. Okay." Emotion tightened his chest and he thought for a moment he'd break. "I thought you were dead."

She smiled up at him, wincing as she tried to sit up. "That was the idea. I wanted her to come close enough so I could grab her. How'd you know she was here?"

"I didn't come for her, Tara. I came for you. I came to tell you I want this to work between us."

A tear ran down her cheek. "I want it to work, too."

Epilogue

Saturday, October 18, 3:00 p.m.

The leaves had turned from green to an array of oranges, browns and yellows and the air had lost its warmth and turned very cool. Winter wasn't far behind.

Three months had passed since Tara's story on Kit had hit the papers. The story had garnered her more attention than she'd imagined and she and her boss, Miriam, had made appearances on network television shows to discuss the case. Miriam was even writing her own book.

The bullet wound in Tara's arm had healed completely and there was no lasting damage.

Mrs. Reston's murder trial was set to begin in early January and Tara had already been assigned to cover it. Pierce had left Boston and secluded himself in his Boca Raton home. He'd refused all interviews.

Tara believed the entire incident had broken the man. For all his faults, Pierce had loved Kit. He'd wanted to build a new life with her, and to discover that she'd only been using him had been too much.

The elevator doors to the homicide floor dinged open. The room still smelled of burnt coffee and the walls remained a dull gray. But catcalls no longer greeted her when she arrived. All the cops knew she and Alex were dating and out of respect for their commander, the detectives kept most whistles to themselves. She still went toe-to-toe with some of the detectives about her headlines, but she wouldn't have had it any other way.

Tara glanced into Alex's office and could see that he faced away from the squad room. He wore a dark turtleneck, which accentuated his broad shoulders and narrow waist. A gun holster hung from his faded jeans. His gaze was dark, pensive.

Her heart swelled. Lord, but she loved that man. She never got tired of looking at him or touching him. Emotion tightened her throat and she had to clear it to regain a sense of composure.

Gertie had been thrilled with their relationship, but his parents and brother were a different matter. To say they were happy would have been an exaggeration. When they'd returned from Europe, Alex had introduced her to them. Everyone was polite, but there was tension. She wasn't their idea of wife material.

But she and Alex were committed to sticking together, no matter what. He'd assured her again and again that she was his family now. And he predicted his parents and brother would come around in time.

Tara knocked on his door and he turned. Immediately, the stern face faded and he smiled as he waved her in. She opened and closed the door softly and stood in front of his desk.

Alex nodded as he listened to his caller. "Great. When you have the forensics report, call me immediately." He hung up the phone, rose and came around to her. There was no hint of a limp anymore and the doctors had said he'd recovered fully.

"Another murder," she said.

"Those fires in the North End weren't set by the guy we arrested. He was cleared."

She frowned. "That's not good."

He shook his head as he helped her with her overcoat. "I don't want to talk about work."

"What do you want to talk about?"

"Us." He kissed her on the lips. "I thought you'd never get here."

She moistened her lips. Her heart thumped in her chest when he touched her. "You said it was important, Detective."

Alex rested his hands on her shoulders. The gesture was casual and intimate, as well. "What are you doing on Christmas Eve?"

She shrugged. "Roxie closes early that day and we usually go to church. Why? Want to join us?"

He grinned as if he knew a big secret. "Church sounds good."

Her eyes narrowed. He was up to something. "You didn't bring me all the way down here to ask me to church, did you?"

"No." He reached in his pocket and pulled out a small velvet box. "This came from the jeweler's this morning. I was going to wait until we saw each other tonight but I just couldn't. That's why I called you."

Tara's breath hitched in her throat as she stared at the small box. "Alex, what have you done?"

Alex looked a little nervous. "Open the box."

Excitement and fear churned inside her. She cracked open the box. Inside was an antique two-carat diamond solitaire set in white gold. "Wow."

"Will you marry me, Tara Mackey?"

The gem caught the light, twisting it into a rainbow of colors. The detail work on the sides was stunningly intricate. "Wow."

"The ring was Gertie's. My grandfather gave it to

her fifty years ago. She offered it to me a couple of weeks ago. She thought it would look good on your hand. I agreed."

Tara opened her mouth to speak but didn't know what to say. The ring was worth more than she earned in a decade. "Wow."

He pulled the ring out of the box and slid it on her ring finger. "Is that a yes?"

Emotion burned in her throat and for a moment she couldn't speak without crying. A tear ran down her cheek. She wrapped her arms around his neck and kissed him on the cheek.

He hugged her hard against him. "That's a definite yes?"

She smiled. "Yes."

From the squad room came a round of cheers. She turned and realized all the detectives had stopped what they were doing and were staring. Each wore a sloppy grin.

"And Christmas Eve works for you?" Alex said.

"Well, yeah, but I don't know anything about planning a wedding. Alex, I'm a disaster when it comes to that kind of thing."

"My mom has agreed to help."

That shocked her. "Your mother has agreed to help? The lady who cringes when I talk a little too loud or speak too candidly about my work—that woman wants to plan the wedding?"

Alex's gaze reflected his own surprise. "The one and the same. It's her way of saying she accepts you."

Tara glanced down at her ring to remind herself that this was real. "She can sure help Roxie." She laughed. "Roxie has started collecting bridal magazines lately.

Alex laughed. "Well that should be interesting. My mother and Roxie planning a wedding."

She grimaced. "They might as well get used to each other."

"As long as you and I get married, that's all I care about."

Smiling, she leaned forward and kissed him. He wrapped his arms around her and relaxed into the kiss.

* * * * *

COMING NEXT MONTH

#1499 CAVANAUGH HEAT—Marie Ferrarella
Cavanaugh Justice
It's been years since Chief of Detectives Brian Cavanaugh has seen his former partner Lila McIntyre, and he's surprised to discover their chemistry is as hot as ever. But he banks down his emotions in order to help Lila catch the stalker who has been harassing her…and discovers a secret that threatens their lives.

#1500 MATCH PLAY—Merline Lovelace
Code Name: Danger
OMEGA undercover agent Dayna Duncan jumps at an undercover assignment overseas. What she doesn't expect is to find former lover USAF pilot Luke Harper awaiting her arrival. A forced reunion may be the only way Dayna and Luke can keep up their aliases, but can they withstand their attraction long enough to complete their mission?

#1501 OUT OF UNIFORM—Catherine Mann
Wingmen Warriors
When Tech Sergeant Jacob "Mako" Stone opens his door to a mysterious woman without a past, he knows his time off is over. As threats to Dee's life bring her and Jacob together, she must set aside her pride and accept the help of the military hero with too many secrets of his own.

#1502 THE PASSION OF SAM BROUSSARD—Maggie Price
Dates with Destiny
A hot lead on a cold case homicide teams up Officer Sam Broussard and OCPD sergeant Liz Scott. Although Sam has never met Liz, there's something very familiar about her. While they uncover the mysteries surrounding the murder, Liz and Sam discover a past neither one remembers sharing...and a killer bent on separating them for eternity.

SRSCNM0108